THE STORY OF MARCEAU MILLER

MARCEAU MILLER

THE STORY OF MARCEAU MILLER

TRANSLATED BY HOWARD CURTIS

BLACK STONE PUBLISHING

Published by special arrangement with Éditions de La Martinière
in conjunction with their duly appointed agent 2 Seas Literary Agency
Published in 2026 by Blackstone Publishing
Cover and book design by Sarah Riedlinger

Printed in the United States of America

First edition: 2026
ISBN 979-8-228-36523-0
Fiction / Thrillers / Suspense

Version 1

Blackstone Publishing
31 Mistletoe Rd.
Ashland, OR 97520

www.BlackstonePublishing.com

Life shrinks or expands in proportion to one's courage.

—Anaïs Nin

PROLOGUE

Like a flash of lightning zigzagging through my brain, a violent blow to my head knocks me off-balance. I'm six hundred feet above the void, climbing a rock face I know well. My nails scratch the granite; my hands lose their grip. At this moment, I realize it's all over. Because I love a challenge, and maybe out of pride, I've always climbed with my bare hands, without a rope. I knew I would pay the price one of these days. First, I see the sky. Then three hundred feet of rock rush past in the blink of an eye. I catch a glimpse of a figure disappearing behind the summit I almost reached. I recognize that figure. It's because of that figure that I'm falling into the void. I'm going to die. One thing is strangely comforting: I'm going to join my sister. She's been gone for twenty years, and when I got up this morning, the last thing I imagined was that I'd be meeting her again today.

My name is Marceau Miller, and I'm a bestselling novelist. Tomorrow, you'll be able to read on my Wikipedia page, just below the line "Born": "Died: May 16, 2021 (aged 40)." By an irony of fate, I've spent years writing as if each day might be my last. I'm leaving behind me the most important manuscript of my life. As if part of me foresaw this moment, my unpredictable appointment with fate. The Grim Reaper doesn't usually send a certified letter to warn you about the day and the hour of your death. I'm leaving that manuscript to them—Sarah and the others. They're free to do what they want with it. I owe them the truth.

My body is floating in the air; I've completely lost control. The ground is approaching at terrifying speed. My heart breaks for my children, Hermione and Benjamin; my wife, Sarah; and the life we built together.

I see my pickup parked at the foot of the rock face, and I realize I'm going to crash to the ground right beside it. Nothing else crosses my mind, even though you're supposed to see your whole life flash by in a situation like this. We've all had this horrible nightmare of falling into blackness, with nothing to stop us. We wake up bathed in sweat, our hearts about to burst, feeling an unease that stays with us for hours.

I've always wondered if the brain switches off before the final impact. In a few hundredths of a second, I'll know for sure.

One hundred and fifty feet.

Thirty feet.

Darkness.

PART ONE:

THE FALL

1

SATURDAY, MAY 15, 2021

THE DAY BEFORE THE DEATH OF MARCEAU MILLER

Sitting in the rocking chair on the terrace of the house, I look up from the novel I've been engrossed in. My tea is still steaming. This is where I like to be, looking out over Lake Geneva, *my* lake—as if it belongs to me. In my husband's books, there's never anything to prepare you for the storm that's about to break over his characters. It often starts insidiously, then strikes with full force. I take a sip of my Saint James, a full-bodied black tea with hints of chocolate, and put down my cup. This is his twentieth book, and he still manages to surprise me. There are things about Marceau I've never been able to figure out, but there's one thing I have to admit: He deserves his success. He handles suspense better than anybody. Maybe even too well. It's everywhere, all the time.

The throb of a motor pulls me from my reading. A boat is approaching the dock at the bottom of the garden. I had it serviced just last week. It's part of the fleet I own with my business partner, Karen. A patched-up little speedboat we'd never dare offer our customers. But our children love it. I sometimes use it to get to the agency, sailing along the shore to Yvoire. It takes fifteen minutes longer than by car, but it's just as practical as Marceau's old pickup for transporting equipment.

Benjamin is at the helm. He's only ten but already maneuvers well. All the same, he's approaching the dock a little too fast. Marceau is waving his arms. He must be asking him to slow down. I'm relieved when the boat glides smoothly to a stop. They've noticed I'm watching. All three wave to me. I smile and wave back. Hermione, our eldest, who's been standing in the bow of the boat, leaps onto the dock and catches the rope her father throws to her. The dock isn't particularly wide. It's supported by long wooden pilings rooted by concrete pillars set deep in a mixture of silt and shingle at the bottom of the lake. Benjamin cuts the motor and joins his father and sister.

I put down my book. I don't even have to mark the page; I can remember it easily: forty. Marceau's age, and mine too. By page forty, things are already starting to look bad for the characters. And I suspect that's just the start.

I stand up, stretch. The shade under the pergola is cool. This terrace was built by my cabinetmaker grandfather—the last work he did before he died suddenly about ten years ago. The wooden exterior of the house, partly covered with flowering vines, gives the place the feel of a vacation getaway. The garden extends almost eighty feet, surrounded by the woods and a hedge that's been abandoned to its own devices. In good weather, thanks to the closeness of the lake, the lawn stays green for a long time. It's freshly mowed and is lined by a fringe of gray sand and pebbles along the shore. I walk toward the children. Benjamin is already starting to tell me about his adventures as he runs toward me, but he's too far away and I can't hear a thing. Hermione is coming up with her father, both carrying the diving gear.

"Dad and I went fifteen feet down! I saw a fish as big as this!"

Even stretched to their full width, my son's arms seem too short for the *huge* fish he saw in the lake. Marceau comes close and kisses me on the forehead. His lips are still cool from the lake. Benjamin pulls him by the sleeve, wanting him to confirm his story about the giant fish.

Hermione creeps up behind him with the cap he dropped and pulls it down over his head, taking him by surprise. For a moment, I feel the fragility of happiness—as fleeting as a fish disappearing into the depths. It makes me dizzy. I become aware of all the things I hold most dear and realize how awful it would be if I lost any of them. Happiness comes to us without warning. It can withdraw just as quickly.

"Sarah?"

Marceau smiles at me. I notice the look in his eyes, and I get the impression he's feeling the same as me. He knows the value of these moments—and how impermanent they are—better than anybody. He's already had to put back together so many broken pieces of happiness. It makes me think of *kintsugi*, the Japanese art of repairing broken pottery.

I can almost trace with my fingers the scars his memories have left on him.

2

SATURDAY, MAY 15, 2021

THE DAY BEFORE THE DEATH OF MARCEAU MILLER

It isn't eight yet, according to the clock in the living room. The noise from outside covers its familiar ticking. In the fading daylight, I can see the lights of several cars filtering through the maples along the drive. The characteristic purr of Alexis's Porsche shakes the glass of the old bookcase my grandmother Louise gave to me. Through the window, I see him getting out of the car, a big smile on his face. Alexis, the same as ever. Benjamin is running around the shiny car. Alexis grabs him and turns him upside down, holding him by the feet like a rag doll. Their laughter makes me smile too. Then they set off at a frenzied run and disappear near the bottom of the garden, shouting and screaming.

Marceau comes down. The stairs are white, the dominant color of our interior. I love light. Thanks to the picture windows looking out to the lake and the reflections of the mountains, we never lose the light. The whole downstairs is open—a modern kitchen leading to a living room and a library. The living room is spacious, maybe a bit too full of furniture, I'm prepared to admit, but comfortable and welcoming.

Marceau joins me on the couch. He takes me in his arms. I know he loves my smile. He smiles back, not taking his eyes off me.

"Are you ready?" I ask.

"You know I'm never really ready for these parties. I'd prefer to slip in between the sheets with you."

I'm touched. This is my favorite time, the days between Marceau finishing one novel and starting the next. It's when I reconnect with him, when we feel the closest.

"Then why are you so eager to repeat this ritual every year when a new novel comes out?"

"Ritual, Sarah, is the key to being a writer. A writer without a ritual is a dead writer."

"Have you turned superstitious? Seriously, what are you scared of? That you'll dry up? That your readers will stop liking you?"

"That's the other thing. A writer who isn't scared is fucked. If he wants to write with passion, he must overcome fear."

"That's a great line, you should keep it for your next interview . . . Talk of the devil, here's your publisher. Early, as usual. He loves these parties, especially my goat-cheese empanadas. Pretty soon we won't be able to see his belt anymore."

Édouard Payet, plump and good-natured, lets his eyes sweep over the front of the house. I know he is reviewing everything. The woodwork, the picture windows, the roof, the small upstairs balcony, the terrace, the casually tended garden. He's always loved this place, the den of his bestselling writer. He knocks at the door, and we let him in. In his wake, Freud, his Welsh corgi, comes running into the hall, which I've cleared of the stuff Benjamin always leaves lying about. Freud's paws skate over the parquet floor. With his short legs and plump body, barking endlessly, he looks just like his master. The two of them eye the food. Already Édouard takes a handful of peanuts. And there I was, wondering where I'd put the bowl. He's obviously found it. In one gesture, he lifts them to his mouth and swallows them whole, like pills. He's a glutton, but he has a hearty smile and the gift of gab.

"Sarah, Marceau! I look forward to this day every year. Nothing ever changes here! And it mustn't—that's the secret of my star writer."

He gives me his usual manly bear hug. I can feel on my shoulder the salt from the peanuts left by his fingers—Freud hasn't had time to lick it off. Édouard suddenly leans over to Marceau, conspiratorially.

"Did you get my little gift?"

I look at Marceau. He seems embarrassed. I have no idea what he's talking about.

"Listen, Édouard, it's fantastic, but I don't have the kind of wrist that's right for a watch. I'd hate myself if I ruined it."

"A Breitling Aviator is perfect for you! You fly your old Savage Bobber almost every week. Marceau, relax! You don't enjoy yourself enough. With the money you make, you should enjoy it!"

"My lakeside house and my plane are all I need. You know me—I want to be prepared if one day it all stops, just like that, without warning."

"I could publish you with my eyes closed, Marceau."

"Don't ever do that."

"Don't worry, I'm not senile yet. And if the book isn't great, Marceau, don't worry, I have some really good ghostwriters."

Marceau's face changes imperceptibly. Édouard has just crossed a line.

"If something was wrong with one of my books . . . it would be the end of me, Édouard."

"Just teasing. I can't wait to see what you have for me, you know that."

I offer Édouard the tray of empanadas while Marceau sneaks out. Freud lifts his muzzle, waiting for crumbs, but Benjamin runs up and distracts him, stroking his head and leading him away, calling his name.

Having scarfed down another mouthful of peanuts with unconcealed satisfaction, Édouard heads to the terrace, where he begins his ritual. He knows I can't bear the smoke in the house. From the inside pocket of his tweed jacket, he takes a case of Spanish cedar and reverently extracts from it a Cohiba Behike 56, the holy grail of cigar connoisseurs.

His gestures are precise, almost religious. First, he gets out his Xikar pocket hygrometer to check the humidity level of the wrapper. Then he rolls the cigar in his expert fingers and sniffs it, inhaling the aroma of leather and precious wood. The engraved silver cigar cutter—a gift from Marceau—makes a clean cut, releasing the first earthy notes. Édouard carefully examines the cut, like a wine expert checking the color of a fine vintage.

His S.T. Dupont lighter produces its characteristic blue flame, and the ritual toasting begins, the flame licking the end of the cigar, preparing the tobacco for lighting. Édouard slowly turns the Cohiba with the precision of a choreographer. The first whiffs rise into the air, bearing the promise of complex aromas to come: notes of roasted coffee, bitter cocoa, and Eastern spices.

A contented smile spreads over his lips as he takes the first puffs, eyes half closed, savoring the moment as if tasting paradise. The imminent success of Marceau's new novel mingles with the ribbons of smoke rising into the night air, dancing above the still waters of the lake.

~

I turn up the stereo, and music fills the house and carries out to the lake. I like to break the silence like this sometimes. I see Karen dancing on the terrace with Hermione and her daughter, Zoé. I didn't see them arrive. Karen is wearing a burnt-orange high-waisted jumpsuit with butterfly sleeves. The material is light, and the plunging neckline shows off her slim figure. The heels she's wearing make her seem tall. I'm suddenly sorry I didn't wear my sexy linen pants. I kiss Karen and wink at her, lightly touching her outfit, and she smiles. Before she's carried off again by the girls, I ask where her husband, Rollin, is. Dancing, she points in the direction of the garden, where Alexis is encouraging Marceau and Rollin, his best friends for twenty years, to show off. Glasses in hand, they start swaying their hips suggestively. Rollin, solid and muscular, is as clumsy as ever, but he follows suit. He's a thoughtful person, warmhearted, the dreamer of the gang, unbeatable when asked about the local flora and fauna during our hikes. A nonconformist to the bone, he's never given up his freedom, scraping a living together with his food truck. On the front steps, Édouard drags on his glowing cigar and blows out wreaths of heavy smoke. His face is lit, his eyes fixed on Marceau. The truth is, at precious moments like this, I'm always scared something bad is going to happen to ruin everything—just like in my husband's novels. There are false alarms, and then there are real tragedies.

10:00 p.m. The automatic sprinkler system comes on. I forgot all about it, and my heart skips a beat. I get a few drops on me. There are cries of amusement and surprise all around. Alexis holds Rollin under the shower, while Marceau hurries to shut off the system. While the three friends fool around, my son pulls me under the water. It's refreshing on a hot early-summer night, and it sobers me up, my heart pounding.

The magic comes to an end as suddenly as it appeared. The sprinkler system is turned off. The boys are soaked. Alexis takes off his clothes and tries to draw Rollin in the direction of the lake, but Rollin resists. He's soaked from head to foot, and he's had enough. Alexis, half naked in the middle of the garden as darkness falls, launches a last appeal, to nobody in particular, then runs across the lawn and dives into the now-dark lake. Several seconds go by before he reappears from the depths in a noisy splash. The movement of the water around him makes the surface of the lake shimmer with points of light. In the distance, the Swiss shoreline looks like an illuminated snake. The temperature of the water is intensely cold, I know. Even after a few drinks, you can't escape its bite. The lake is dangerous. One time when I was young, I almost drowned, which is why I decided to become a better swimmer. I even have a few medals to prove it.

Rollin's clothes are sticking to his skin, revealing his brawny shoulders. "I need a towel," he says.

I laugh. "You're crazy, why don't you take some things from Marceau's closet? They may be a bit tight, but better than nothing."

Karen and I laugh as Rollin goes into the house. We've known each other for a long time, through our husbands. Our friendship and mutual trust made it possible for us to set up our boat rental agency, which is doing pretty well these days. A few yards from the shore, Alexis whistles and throws his soaked underpants in the direction of the garden. Freud catches the wet rag mid-flight and carries it to his master. Alexis emerges from the water backward, his white buttocks turned toward us.

Karen is the first to react.

"Alexis, the children! You really are too much!"

Alexis continues regardless. He reaches the dock, then jumps back in the lake, hamming it up, pretending to be clumsy. Benjamin also starts to undress, but I stop him. Disappointed, he walks down to the water and urges Alexis on. From a distance, Alexis tries to persuade me to come in, but he's wasting his time.

Rollin reappears, wearing Marceau's clothes. He has a strange look on his face. Is he tired? He's lost his smile, that's for sure. He carries a big towel to rescue his naked buddy, who's just come out of the water and is starting to shiver.

They move away together to the end of the garden, near the trees at the edge of the woods, not far from the boat. It looks like they're in deep conversation. I hope nothing's wrong. The special thing about these parties is how they take us back twenty years, to a time when we were a lot more carefree. Now Marceau comes out of the house, looking serious, as if he's somewhere else—that worried expression he has every now and again. Why tonight? The few times I've tried to understand Marceau's moods, I found myself alone on the edge of a precipice over a bottomless pit. It's a boundary I don't cross, a rule we don't talk about, a distance there for his protection.

~

It's after midnight, and the swimming episode has changed the atmosphere. Freud's barking attracts attention. His hair is on end, and he stands facing the small wood adjacent to the garden. Édouard whistles to him, but he finally has to go fetch him. The area around the house is full of nocturnal animals.

Édouard comes back with Freud in his arms. He thanks me for the party and reminds Marceau of the schedule for the coming days. He's appearing on a major literary TV program and is supposed to record a radio ad. The press agent will send him an updated schedule for the various bookstore signings. What I've learned over the years is that I share my husband with Édouard, the journalists, the readers . . . but also with lots of fictional characters. If they could all go away and leave me a bit more of Marceau, I'd feel a lot better. Closing his computer briefly on a manuscript in progress isn't enough. But I'm not the one who decides, and I'm not sure he decides either.

~

By 1:45 a.m., everybody has gone home. Hermione and Benjamin are finally in their rooms, totally bushed. I knock discreetly at the door of Marceau's study, his sanctuary.

"Give me five more minutes. I'm just writing something, and then I'll be with you."

In my head I translate: half an hour, an hour. I head to the bathroom and take an Advil. I'm tired and I'm sure the booze is going to give me a headache. Even though I'm exhausted, I'm pleased the party was a success. As I slip between the sheets, I feel myself float away, but I resist. I don't like falling asleep without the warmth of Marceau beside me. I need him. I try to hold off sleep a bit longer, but I finally drift off.

3

SUNDAY, MAY 16, 2021

THE DAY OF THE DEATH OF MARCEAU MILLER

5:10 a.m. Hazy light. Marceau isn't next to me. Fucking writers! I'm pissed, but my eyes close and I plunge back to sleep.

~

8:15 a.m. A slight headache. Even with the shutters closed, I can tell the weather is good. The light hurts. On Marceau's side of the bed, the sheets aren't even creased. Did he sleep in his study or what? I creep down the hall, trying not to wake Hermione and Benjamin. Marceau isn't in his study, but I don't go inside. To be honest, I hardly ever set foot in there—he doesn't like it.

Half-awake, I try to remember if he told me anything, but nothing comes to mind. He should be here with me. The living room is a mess. I pick up a few things left from the party and look out into the garden. Nobody there. I go onto the terrace, barefoot, facing the lake. It's calm, untroubled by any wind. The temperature is mild. Our speedboat is still tied up at the dock. Facing the hangar in the distance, I can't see our old pickup. I am pretty sure it was parked there yesterday. I walk around the back of the house. The cold grass absorbs my steps and tickles the soles of my feet. The hangar is wide open, as usual. Marceau's plane is there with its gleaming propeller and broad wings. If he took it, I would have heard it taking off from the adjacent meadow, but the pickup is still nowhere to be found. I look toward the woods and the path leading to the road. I call Marceau, my voice rough from sleep, but all it does is stir a bird, which rises above the house, beating its wings. For a moment I envy the bird, flying above the world, with a view over the lake and the mountains. From up there, can it see Marceau?

Back in the house, I find Marceau's sneakers in the hall closet next to mine and his coats, but his climbing bag is empty. His climbing shoes and magnesium bags are not there. I'm upset for a moment, but then I remember he got rid of them, the day he promised to stop climbing without a rope, without any security . . . and above all, without care. The fact that he didn't take anything with him means he'll be back soon. I send him a text, reminding him that we have to synchronize our schedules, his book events and, on my side, the boat business, which never lets up at this time of year. Not to mention the children, who aren't old enough to take care of themselves.

~

Noon. I'm irritably peeling potatoes for the fries Benjamin has demanded. And for the tenth time at least, I tell the children no, I don't know where their father is. Marceau has never been good at keeping promises. Hermione was counting on him to install her smart lighting system, and Benjamin to help him assemble his new radio-controlled plane. I suggest they find other things to fill their time. No new message on my cell phone. I call for the third time. "Hello, you've reached Marceau Miller . . ." I hang up. By the fifth text, my tone has changed.

Where the fuck are you?

4

MONDAY, MAY 17, 2021

THE DAY AFTER THE DEATH OF MARCEAU MILLER

8:00 a.m. I call for Benjamin one more time.

"If you don't come down now, you'll have to go to school without breakfast."

Hermione is being difficult as usual. Just asking her to clear the table is enough for her to curse and slam the door of her room. In other words, a normal Monday morning. Almost normal. Usually, Marceau irritates Hermione before I do.

Last night, I told them a lie, maybe the first of many. Dad had to go traveling for the launch of his new novel. He'd mentioned it to me, and I'd forgotten all about it. I haven't yet started calling our friends and acquaintances. I'm desperately clinging to the hope that Marceau will show up with an explanation I haven't thought of and everything will go back to normal.

~

8:15 a.m. There's a bitter taste in my throat, and the stress is killing my stomach. I search for pills in the bathroom cabinet, but I don't find anything that hasn't expired. I tell myself I'll be fine as soon as I have any news. I hurry to get ready, trying not to forget anything—it's a workday after all.

I'm late and in no mood for the usual office emergencies. Karen is already dealing with the first customers. Obviously, I look stressed out, and she asks if everything's OK and what I did on Sunday. I can't help it and tell her I haven't heard from Marceau since Saturday night, after the party. Does she have any idea where he might be? I see surprise in her eyes. I must seem really out of it. She hesitates, searching for a reassuring explanation. Maybe it's something to do with the publication of his book? That doesn't hold water, I say. He would have left me a note, even if he wanted to go off to be alone, as he sometimes does. I pace around the office as if I'm searching here too. Karen makes me a cup of tea and looks at the list of our available boats while I count them one by one, moored at the agency's dock. Occasionally, Marceau has borrowed one, as have Alexis and Rollin. Karen calls Rollin, while I try my luck with Alexis. My heart beats faster as the hope I've been clinging to starts to drop away. They don't know anything. Next, I try his publisher. Édouard reminds me of Marceau's TV and radio engagements, but otherwise he has nothing to add. One dead end after another, even after contacting a slew of friends of friends. My knuckles are white from clutching my phone. Alarms are going off in my head. I can see the same barely disguised anxiety in Karen's eyes. She assures me she can run the agency and almost pushes me out the door. I have more important things to do. I have to find Marceau.

I've always been able to count on Karen. We understand each other perfectly—we laugh at the same things, don't make snap judgments, and put up with each other's faults. True partners with enormous trust in each other. She could take everything from me if she wanted, and I'd turn a blind eye. Setting up the agency on the lake was one of the best decisions I've ever made. My place is here, on the lake, surrounded by the forests and mountains. It is my kingdom and my roots.

But Marceau is also part of my roots. Leaving without warning, without answering the phone, especially when his new book is coming out, isn't normal. It's like I'm being asked to grope my way forward in the dark, with nothing to hold on to. My heart skips a beat every time I get a text or call, more and more of them, from people we know. They're all as anxious as I am; they ask me if there's any news, occasionally make suggestions. They obviously have their own thoughts, but they keep them to themselves.

~

3:20 p.m. I come home after driving along the shore of the lake, from Yvoire to Meillerie and all the way to the Swiss border. I stopped everywhere—the restaurants, gyms, all the places, some quite remote, where Marceau goes when he wants to escape from everything and write. I am doing what I can, but I realize I need help and park outside the police station in Thonon-les-Bains.

My stomach's in knots. What the fuck am I doing here? A young officer listens to my story and takes notes of everything I say. He tries to reassure me. There's no reason to be alarmed. He asks questions about my marriage. Do we quarrel? Have either of us been unfaithful? I remind him that the reason I came to the police station is because I don't have any explanation as to why he's gone. He asks me to calm down. Did I need to raise my voice?

Eventually, Captain Robin Delmas introduces himself. I can tell he's arrogant and is looking at me with scorn. In his office I tell him the whole story over again, stage by stage—the party, the drinking, yes, there was drinking, but nothing else, definitely not! I find it hard to keep my voice down. I'm so close to losing my temper, I can barely speak. Who does he think we are? Among celebrities, he maintains, drugs are common, and this time I really do fly off the handle. No, Marceau doesn't touch cocaine. The last time either of us smoked a joint was in college. The patronizing look on his face is testing my patience. Did Marceau leave a note? Is anything missing in the house? No. Any warning signs? Any particular change in his habits recently? I've already asked myself these questions. I say no for what seems like the hundredth time. I can hardly breathe. All I know is that he left in the pickup.

Since he's been gone for less than forty-eight hours, Delmas says, the police can't launch a search for him yet—not for a forty-year-old of sound mind with no specific problems and no reasons to leave. And that's it. He looks me up and down. I feel like hitting him. Clearly, he doesn't think there's a reason for concern. Whatever I say, I get the feeling he won't hear me. There's nothing more to do. He shows me to the door.

I feel worse when I leave than I did when I arrived. I am having a hard time breathing; I feel empty and alone. Misunderstood, gaslit, but still determined. This Delmas guy hasn't seen the last of me. My mind is working overtime. There has to be something else . . . Then an idea flashes through my mind. I climb back into my car and set off like a shot.

5

MONDAY, MAY 17, 2021

THE DAY AFTER THE DEATH OF MARCEAU MILLER

Thonon-les-Bains is in my rearview mirror, though Captain Delmas's infuriating voice is still echoing in my head. I want to drive fast, but the traffic on the main road is gridlocked. I turn off onto secondary roads, closer to the lake. I won't save any time this way, but at least I can drive more freely. The view of the lake is revealed in the gaps between the ash, beech, and maple trees. At least the lake never lets me down. I drive fast past houses with tiled roofs burnished by time, occasionally tinged with the tender green of moss. I'm almost home. The familiar landscape is both comforting and cruelly empty. My heart is still pounding, wavering between the hope Marceau will be home and the chilling fear that he'll still be missing.

There's a car parked outside the house, though I can barely make it out through the hedge. I speed up on the rutted dirt road, leaving a trail of brown dust that covers the leaves of the trees. Is Marceau home? I'm so overwhelmed by anxiety, a tingling sensation runs through my body. Everything feels out of my control, and I have a strange premonition that something has happened.

A man suddenly emerges from the woods, waving his arms at me. I realize I'm driving much too fast. I slam on the brakes, stopping right near the man, who wipes dust from his face. It's Reynaud. He looks upset. I realize that the SUV in the driveway is his. Although my hopes of seeing Marceau are dashed, seeing him here is a comfort. Yves Reynaud knows me as well as he knows Marceau—he's known both of us since we were teenagers. He's also a retired policeman. He's solid as a rock and doesn't look his age, which is seventy. We don't see each other often, but it's always as if no time has passed. He's always been there, unfailingly loyal, a father figure. He walks around my car and climbs in the passenger side. I can't speak; I'm sure I look distraught. He leans over and hugs me. Suddenly, it's all too much. I bite my lip so I don't cry. On his shirt I feel the heat of summer and the smell of the forest, just like I do on Marceau's clothes when he comes back from his long walks. Reynaud was born here; it's always been his home. I cling to him as if Providence has sent him to help me.

"Tell me the whole story, Sarah, from the beginning. What's going on with Marceau?"

I see in him the concern of a friend, eager to reassure, ready to do anything to help, and also the reflexes of a former policeman. At least he listens to me, and the old fox knows the area like the back of his hand. I tell the story one more time. Just saying the word *case* terrifies me. Everything that's happening takes us back twenty years, digs up memories I don't want to remember. I refuse to remember. I know Reynaud is thinking about it as well. I start the car again, more calmly this time, and park in front of the house.

I take Reynaud to the garden shed.

"What are you looking for, Sarah?"

I open the plastic chests where we keep our diving gear. I rummage through the clutter on the workbench that serves as a desk. Marceau comes here from time to time, but all I find are papers and tools, nothing to grab my attention. I bring my fist down, sending a set of screwdrivers flying. Reynaud takes the heavy wooden trays from the shelves. I ask him to be careful—they're full of nails, screws, and spikes. One of the trays is empty, but before he puts it back, I rub my fingers over the bottom. A thin film sticks to my index and middle fingers. I sniff it. It's magnesium, which the powder climbers use on their hands to help their grip. Reynaud and I exchange looks.

"He promised me he'd stop," I say, but I can't go on.

I feel like crying, but nothing comes, as if breaking down would confirm the worst has happened. I'm scared I already know. All it took was a fine, almost imperceptible trace of powder. Secrets never stay hidden. Reynaud puts his calloused hands on my shoulders, and his expression changes. He lowers his eyes before he speaks.

"Listen, Sarah, Marceau and I have been seeing each other from time to time."

I free myself from his embrace. "What do you mean? Without me? Why? He never told me."

"We're all driven by old demons."

My blood freezes. The door to my worst memories creaks open. Images flash through my mind, and I push them away. I can't stand the pain. It's like I'm a child about to get a shot. She was my best friend twenty years ago. She was Marceau's sister, born the same year as him, less than a year between them. We were inseparable.

I stare at Reynaud for a long time before asking, "You're talking about Jade, aren't you?"

"It was my case. I don't know where we screwed up."

I feel the ground giving way beneath my feet. "Where is he? Say something, for fuck's sake!"

"I have no idea, Sarah, no idea . . . but I sometimes saw him near the . . ."

"Near the fucking place where Jade disappeared, in the mountains, is that it? Why stir it all up? Do you know how much it hurts?"

It's all coming back. And it's too much for me.

6

MONDAY, MAY 17, 2021

THE DAY AFTER THE DEATH OF MARCEAU MILLER

Reynaud's SUV is speeding along the mountain road in the direction of the border between France and Switzerland, less than twenty-five miles away. On the narrow D25, between woods and forests, we pass through quiet villages, where the houses with their exposed woodwork and broad roofs seem to have been there forever, like picture postcards from our grandparents' day. After Sciez, we continue on the D1005, the road that leads to Switzerland. Reynaud drives fast, passing other cars, and he's silent, concentrating. After Évian, we drive along the lake, the snowcapped Alps in the distance. As we continue, the hills turn into mountains. We pass Lugrin, then the border at Saint-Gingolph. I send Karen a text, asking if she can look after Benjamin until I get back. I haven't been to the exact place we're going in years, even though Marceau and I sometimes hike in the area. We've always shared a love of nature, of forests and mountains, but right now the vastness around us is making me dizzy.

The road becomes increasingly rough, and I hang on for dear life. As we gain altitude, my eardrums start to pop. As the road gets narrower and narrower, like the source of a stream, we slow to a crawl. We pass the La Planche parking lot, the last still accessible to cars. Reynaud continues to a bend in the road, a few hundred yards from Switzerland, and then cuts through the trees, driving over fallen branches. Staying in first gear, he pushes the vehicle until we can't get any farther. We're at an altitude of almost six thousand feet, about forty minutes' walk from Lake Neuteu. We look at each other. Reynaud takes out a flask, which he puts in a backpack, and his walking poles. This is the first stage, the easy part. Around us, the forest, and not just any forest, either for me or for Reynaud. I exhale and set off after Reynaud, who is already many yards ahead. The climb is treacherous, and I have to watch where I'm walking to avoid the traps laid by the mountains. I'm starting to feel heat in my thighs and calves, and there's a veil of sweat on my face. Lake Neuteu appears in front of us, surrounded by sharp mountain peaks and forest as far as the eye can see—and unbearable memories. I try to ignore the images that flash through my mind, but the anxiety doesn't go away. Time has not healed the pain deep inside me.

~

Galvanized by fear, I've overtaken Reynaud, and I'm the first to get there, my eyes like lasers searching the perimeter of the isolated lake, more than two hundred yards long and almost a hundred wide. There isn't another soul in sight. The best vantage point for a loner like Marceau is just over a half mile away, the highest peak around here, a sheer monster of rock. This is no pleasure hike; it's only for people who know the mountains. Reynaud catches up with me. I think about the magnesium we found in the garden shed, and a shiver runs down my spine. Reynaud tells me the name of the peak.

The Dent du Vélan.

I feel a tightness in my stomach.

"It's against the law to climb here, isn't it?"

Reynaud pauses for a moment, his silence chilling.

"There are a few abandoned paths, I think . . ."

We continue, turning our back on Lake Neuteu, gradually ascending toward the Dent du Vélan. We help each other up the rockiest, steepest part of the trail, and sweat is trickling down my back. There's sweat on Raynaud's face too.

Three-quarters of an hour without taking a break.

"We're almost there."

My left eardrum is killing me, and we're still gaining altitude. We turn for a moment to see Lake Geneva, vast in the distance.

"Marceau always loved the lake."

The setting sun creates shadows between the rocks, creating a play of light and dark in the austere landscape. Suddenly, my sight is drawn to a patch of color between two stunted trees. I shield my eyes with my hand to see better. Anxiety rises in me like a wave, and without thinking I start running as fast as the uneven terrain will let me.

"MARCEAU!!!"

I call his name over and over again, as loudly as I can, but there is only the echo of my own voice. I throw off my backpack so I can go faster, and fall, grazing my hands on the rocks. Behind me, I hear Reynaud's muffled voice.

"Be careful, Sarah!" he calls, but I don't listen to him.

I bend to pick up the blue I saw through the trees. It's Marceau's old sports bag, one he almost never used, torn as if an animal has ripped it apart. Instinctively, I sniff the bag. It smells like Marceau. I feel dizzy, and as I look around, I see a flash of light. It's the windshield of Marceau's pickup, parked next to a rock that almost completely conceals it. *How did it get here?*

Reynaud catches up to me, out of breath. Marceau must have come from the Swiss side, he says. It's pretty risky to get here in a pickup. *A ridiculous risk.* And a long way around. But I've moved away, calling

Marceau's name, looking in every direction, taking in the whole area, looking for a higher point where I can get a better view.

That's when I glimpse a dark shape, slumped among the stones a few yards away, laid like an offering at the foot of the pitiless rock face. It's Marceau, *my* Marceau, lying motionless and alone, surrounded by stone and blood. I fall to my knees near his body, ready to embrace him and scream at him too, but Reynaud holds me back and pulls me to him instead. I struggle to find some explanation, but there isn't any. Marceau lost his footing and fell. I can't believe it. I'd like to wake up from this nightmare, but it's all too real. Pain explodes inside me.

"Damn it, Marceau, why? Why have you done this to us?" My screams are stifled against Reynaud's shirt as I pound his chest with pointless blows.

~

Minutes have passed—or maybe hours, I've lost track of time. The first hysterical moments of grief have passed, and now I'm in shock. The silence is deafening. I turn to look at Marceau's body again and fix the image in my memory. Covered in dust, streaked with black, clotted blood. Broken limbs. Eyes staring up at the sky, as if he wanted to take in the sight of the mountain peaks. Everything within me comes to a standstill. I can't get my head around it. My life, my family, all the things I've built, the father of my children. It's all come to a shuddering halt. Reynaud gently turns me away from looking at the disturbing sight of Marceau's body. All kinds of questions are buzzing in my head. Is this really happening? What am I going to do? What do I tell Benjamin and Hermione?

Reynaud is trying to talk to me, but I can't absorb what he is saying. I'm in a bubble: The noise of the world is muted as if it's from a long way away. Dazed, overwhelmed. Reynaud is waving his phone at me. I try to come back to reality. There's no signal here, we can't reach anyone, and we're completely isolated from the rest of the world. With Reynaud leading the way, we climb back down. I see without seeing, feel without feeling. What shocks me is that Marceau is gone. I can't accept it, and yet . . . I'm leaving him up there, just long enough to call for help . . . But what good is help now?

There's no signal around Lake Neuteu either. In a heavy silence, we continue until we get to the SUV. Turning to look again at the mountains, I demand explanations—I want to understand.

~

Closer to Lake Geneva, our phones at last have a signal. I've got tons of messages and texts. Reynaud parks the truck and calls Captain Delmas's number. He reports what we've discovered, and hearing the words out loud hurts me. After the call, Reynaud is ready to take me home, but I want to be back up in the mountains with Marceau. I want to be up there with Marceau for as long as possible. I can't be anywhere else. Reynaud does a U-turn.

~

As we climb back to the Dent du Vélan, bruised and exhausted, a police helicopter flies overhead. I feel the wind from its blades above us as we reach Marceau's body. Delmas, another officer, and a man who must be a medical examiner climb out of the helicopter. These scenes feel familiar—the kind Marceau describes in his novels. The men walk over to my husband's body, analyze the scene, speculate, look up at the peak of the Dent du Vélan, then down at Lake Geneva in the valley. I answer their questions, and this time they take me seriously. No, no conflicts in our marriage or family, nothing abnormal in any way. And Marceau was definitely not doing drugs. He was a hypochondriac; he wouldn't take any of that shit, even when prescribed by a doctor. The thought of losing control terrified him. The medical examiner cuts short the questioning—he'll know more after the postmortem, he says. But if I know

Marceau, he won't find anything. I can't stand their suspicions, and I'm ready to leap at their throats if I have to. Reynaud places his hand on my arm. He's right—it isn't worth it.

I stop to observe the scene, just the way Marceau would have described it. A corpse, a medical examiner, police officers. And one detail that doesn't fit.

Marceau would have seen it too.

Reynaud is looking at me curiously—and so is the medical examiner.

"If my husband fell on his back," I say, "how come there's a wound on his face?"

Marceau always finished his chapters with that kind of explosive detail.

Delmas and the medical examiner exchange glances. Reynaud frowns.

"Madame Miller," Delmas says in that condescending tone I hate, "this isn't one of your husband's novels. The cause of death was definitely the fall. Almost fifteen hundred feet, at first glance."

Reynaud looks up at the rock face, doubtful.

"She's right, a body that falls doesn't bounce."

Delmas walks over to Reynaud.

"Tell me, we know you're a retired policeman, but are you also a pathologist?"

Reynaud's face clouds over.

Ignoring the back-and-forth, the medical examiner speaks again.

"A body falling from such a height would generate enormous kinetic energy. When it hits the ground, it would flatten like a ripe fruit and cause massive internal damage. It may indeed be unusual to find a lesion like this on the opposite side of the body. Right now, there's nothing to explain it."

Reynaud hasn't taken his eyes off Delmas, and they drive home his point.

"It's called experience. And when you don't have enough of it, you can screw up an investigation."

7

THURSDAY, MAY 20, 2021

THE DAY OF MARCEAU'S FUNERAL

The sun is bright in the sky, the heat intense. The kind of day Marceau loved, an ideal day for getting away, for writing far from everything in the silence of nature. Under the noonday sun, the water of the lake is crystal clear. Instead, here he is at the cemetery in Yvoire, enclosed in a coffin, ready to vanish beneath the earth. At least the coffin is made of high-quality wood from the surrounding forests, carved and polished. I don't know what he wanted. We never really talked about it. I wanted something private, for him, for me, for the children. About thirty people, family and close friends. Dressing in black on such a beautiful day feels strange.

The priest chooses his words carefully—I didn't have the strength to suggest anything to him. Benjamin and Hermione cling to me. The pressure of their bodies against mine and their tears force me to face what's happened. Benjamin's fingers dig into me, his face buried in my dress, barely able to breathe. He doesn't want to see anything. Hermione looks tired and lost. The last traces of her childhood, her innocence, have left her. They say hardship makes us strong, but right now it's breaking us. My life has been turned upside down in a few days. This morning, I threw up the meds the doctor prescribed to calm me. I have to keep going, for Benjamin and Hermione at least.

Édouard insisted on hiring a security firm to keep the reporters and onlookers away. They're doing their job: no pests, no flashbulbs, no questions. The coffin sinks beneath the earth. Goodbye, Marceau . . . Ahead of me, an empty horizon without him. Alexis and Rollin support me. Karen is unable to hold back her tears, and others in the gathering are also crying. Reynaud hugs me—his eyes are red too—and in a hoarse voice, he says, "I'm here for you."

Through my tears I spot Captain Delmas. I indicate to Rollin and Alexis that I can stand now. I gently try to loosen Benjamin's fingers, but he clings even harder. I ask Karen for help. My poor boy can hardly breathe. He's ashen faced, distraught. Karen puts her arms around him. I walk over to Delmas, who's sizing everyone up.

"I'll give you a list, if it makes it any easier for you. By the way, you weren't on it."

"My condolences, Madame Miller."

Just for today, he's put aside the arrogance.

"How is the investigation going?"

"That's what I'm here for, Madame Miller."

Maybe I was too hasty about his arrogance. Or maybe it's just that his expression changes as soon as he hears the words *investigation* or *case.* I want clues, I want answers.

"Marceau wasn't alone up there, I'm sure of it. It's your job to find out who was there."

He looks away. "The medical examiner isn't sure of anything. But what my team has discovered so far does point to it being an accident."

"So why are you here? To make up the numbers? To play at being a good cop even though you don't have a thing? Reynaud's right."

"This may not be the right time, Madame—"

"I didn't get to choose the time!"

"I think you know what I mean. I'm just doing my job."

I turn my back on him. I can't bear the sight of him a moment longer. I look out over the lake. I wish the surface would tear; I wish my anger could rip it open. In the distance, the mountains rise, stern and immutable, indifferent witnesses to our drama. Their peaks vanish in a light mist like a veil. The unremitting sun taunts me. The dance of shadow and light on the surface of the lake brings to mind the dark areas in our past, the flashes of truth that Marceau's death has cast, a truth I'm determined to reconstruct, whatever the cost.

8

TUESDAY, JUNE 1, 2021
TWO WEEKS AFTER MARCEAU'S DEATH

It's like time is standing still. Or I am. As if I've received a blow and I'm stunned. Every time I open the door, I have the feeling Marceau is waiting for me there, in the entrance, looking at me in that way he had that I could never quite figure out. But all that's left of him is his aviator jacket, hanging from a peg in the hall. I stroke the material and sniff the lining, where his scent still lingers. Since the tragedy, when my friends have come to visit, I've seen them looking furtively at the jacket, not daring to put their coats on top of it. I just want to believe that none of this ever happened. That jacket, with climbing clips in the pockets, is Marceau. My Marceau. I hear the engine of a tourist plane above the lake. Instinctively, I lean out the window to watch it pass, but its tail doesn't look anything like the tail of Marceau's plane. It isn't him. It will never be him again.

Marceau still climbed in secret, and he also flew to exorcise the terrible, abrupt loss of his father thirty years ago. It happened on a Sunday. Of course it wasn't Marceau who told me the story. I read about the accident in a newspaper, which he had kept. His father's Savage Bobber crashed into the lake at exactly 3:32 p.m. According to an amateur sailor who was on the lake at the time, the plane had presented signs of distress as it was approaching the flying club. It passed about 150 feet over his boat and then plunged into the lake.

"It all happened very quickly"—these words underlined in pencil. The Savage Bobber had been seen a few minutes earlier above Morzine, and it had then flown over the mountains of Avoriaz and climbed back up to Abondance before passing Thonon and Évian.

Since the accident, Marceau sometimes visited the wreck, nearly a hundred feet down at the bottom of the lake. I never told anyone, except my friend and partner, Karen. The fact is, Marceau had his secrets, secrets that made him mysterious, sometimes taciturn and distant. Especially when he was writing, stuck in his bubble with his characters. Sometimes when I was talking to him, I had the impression he didn't hear me. Was he deliberately putting distance between us? Our daily routines, especially those involving the children, had gradually eaten away at our initial passion, but we were still happy. Marceau's sudden death has wrecked me. The world that used to be reassuring, *my* world, collapsed two weeks ago, and I'm left to face the ruins of it alone.

Alone, because there's nothing to fill the hole. The shoulder I could always lean on is gone. Though we've shared everything for years, even Karen can't do anything. I met Karen a year after Jade's disappearance, and we became friends right away, as if I'd transferred to her my symbiotic attachment to Jade. A few years later, we became partners and set up Lake Geneva Nautical, a small agency for renting and repairing boats. It was tough at first, but we could count on the boys—Marceau, Alexis, and Rollin—for support. We managed to balance the books and even to keep a reasonable cash flow. I was determined to be independent, even though Marceau's income could easily have been enough for us. Boat hire is a tough line of work on Lake Geneva. There's a lot of competition. Karen has been handling the business for the two of us since I started foundering. I don't even know how she could help me—nobody can. It's a struggle every day to come to terms with my new life, a life without Marceau.

I quicken my pace as I walk up the drive to the mailbox. The air caresses my skin, but I don't feel any pleasure in it. Spring has awakened the garden from its winter torpor. Everything is a bright green that exudes happiness, but it feels strange to be happy without Marceau. The lawn is overgrown, and the branches of the lime tree Marceau promised to cut have invaded the road. There's a lot of mowing and pruning to be done, and I can't bear the thought of it. I'm wearing the same clothes I wore yesterday. My jeans and sweatshirt are still pretty clean, but my sneakers are splattered with mud. I wandered around outside the house again last night. It's been happening a lot since Marceau died. I can't sleep. There are too many nightmares.

The mail is overflowing from the box again today, just as it has been every day for the last two weeks. The mailbox has come loose on one side and sways slightly. The other morning, I'd finally had enough of condolence letters, and I started hitting the mailbox, again and again, and screamed. The mailbox finally gave way when I reversed the pickup and drove over it. From the kitchen window, I saw the postman put it back up the next day. He didn't say anything.

I empty the damned box and walk back to the house with my haul. This house, left to us by my grandmother Louise, was our pride and joy. Warm and filled with light, with wide bay windows looking out onto the garden. A paradise on the shore of Lake Geneva, facing the immensity of the mountains between Switzerland and France. A paradise that now feels empty.

I slam the door behind me and throw the mail onto the coffee table in the living room. The letters spread across the surface of the table, rare, expensive Cuban mahogany. Marceau didn't skimp when he bought that table—the price was embarrassingly high. Seeing my name over and over again on the envelopes is unbearable. Sarah, Sarah, Sarah . . . All I want to do is forget, even though everything reminds me of Marceau. Like that graceful model sailboat on the old burnished-wood art deco cabinet.

Marceau made that boat just before Benjamin was born. My mind wanders for a moment, and I see myself on a boat in the middle of an ocean. The boat drifts, then disappears beyond the horizon and sinks. This vision reflects exactly what I'm feeling: the sense that I'm sinking, drowning.

My gaze wanders toward the bookcase on the wall between the two bay windows. Marceau loved reading as much as he loved writing. My eyes linger over the bottle of whisky behind the glass front of the bookcase. It's been there for ages. A gift from his publisher on the occasion of his first big hit, ten years ago. I can still remember the magazine cover with the tagline "Who is Marceau Miller, the novelist who sells millions of copies?" illustrated by a photograph of Marceau staring at the camera with an enigmatic smile. The blue of his irises was more pronounced than it was in real life—presumably retouched by the magazine's photographic department.

I don't know why, but that bottle, a Dalmore 1980, was Marceau's prized possession. He never wanted to open it. Well, I'm going to! The glass door is locked. I try to force the lock, but it resists. I want it, that rare ten-thousand-euro bottle of 51.2-proof whisky from one of the oldest distilleries in the Highlands, aged in sherry casks. That's what Marceau's publisher announced proudly to the guests the evening of the party. I remember finding it pretentious.

"Everyone's going to want a piece of you now, but if you follow my advice, I'll help you keep a cool head," he said, with a glance at me.

Let's see if this single malt is capable of deadening my pain. I'm not going to let a fucking lock stop me. I want to break things. I grab a cloth from the kitchen, wrap it around my hand, and hit the glass with my fist, putting all of my weight behind it. The glass shatters, and pieces scatter across the rug, under the furniture, and over the parquet floor. I turn, breathless, to make sure nobody has caught me in the act. I'm alone; the children are at school. And there's no risk now of Marceau coming out of his study, angry with the mess I've made.

I grab the bottle by the neck and retreat a few steps. The shards of glass have made a huge scratch on the floor. It feels good to destroy the beautiful parquet, and I hold back a nervous laugh. I try to open the bottle, but the cap won't turn. I struggle with it until my hand hurts, then wedge it between my knees, until at last it opens. I grab a glass from the shelf and pour myself a draft of whisky. The fumes of alcohol are so strong they make me feel dizzy, and I have to stop myself from falling. I drink the glass in one go, then pour myself another.

I stare at the envelopes scattered across the table. I don't yet have the courage to either open them or throw them straight in the garbage. One of them attracts my attention. It doesn't look like the dozens of letters of condolences I've received since Marceau died. I pull it out of the pile of mail and notice, printed in the top right-hand corner, the logo of HSBC. This correspondence is from their branch based in Geneva, although we don't have an account there. Could our financial adviser have been hiding something from me? What do these HSBC sharks want? Money? I open the envelope. It contains a letter from the bank and another envelope without any name on it. Intrigued, I take another gulp of whisky and start to read.

Madame, allow me to express my sincerest condolences on behalf of HSBC. I am writing to inform you that your late husband opened an account in our establishment, of which I am the manager, and that he had a safety-deposit box. In addition, he entrusted me with this envelope, which he asked me to convey to you in the event that he died prematurely. In conformity with his wishes, I therefore ask you to please accept . . .

I don't even bother to finish the letter but feverishly tear open the envelope. A shiver runs down my spine. I recognize Marceau's handwriting immediately. I can hardly breathe, and my hands are shaking. Marceau and his secrets . . . Suddenly, I have a bad feeling.

Sarah, Alexis, Rollin,

If you are receiving this letter, it's probably because my crazy passion for climbing mountains with my bare hands, without rope or harness, will have got the better of me and I will have missed a handhold on one of the rock faces I so much loved to scale. I was aware of the risks I was taking. You know me, I've always believed you can't put a price on freedom. I can imagine the immense grief that must be yours at this moment. Sarah, in particular. I'm so sorry, really. Even more because of what I have to tell you now. The reason I haven't told you about this before is that . . . quite simply, I couldn't. The secret I have carried all these years links the four of us.

I can hear his voice as if he's beside me reading this letter himself. I think of Rollin and Alexis, who must also have received it by now. They, too, must be thinking: *Jade.* Everything starts with Jade, and everything always leads back to Jade . . . Marceau's sister. My best friend. We were twenty years old.

August 14, 2001. A Tuesday. How can I forget that day? Paradoxically, I think it was that day that I discovered my vocation as a writer. Escape as a refuge, as if, in inventing my stories, I could find answers to the questions that would haunt me from then on in my life. The successes I've had, one after the other, are closely linked in my mind to the shock we suffered that day, the shock that set everything in motion. You all remember, obviously. Forgive me for reminding you once again of what happened. But there is a part of this story that I alone have carried, all this time.

Forgive me.

That hike in the forest, Jade leaving before us, leaving us far behind. Her disappearance. The fruitless police search that went on for days. The mountains had taken our Jade, had taken her body and left not the slightest trace. My little sister, whom I had been unable to protect. We couldn't resign ourselves to accepting the inevitable. You remember, as I do, those days we spent scouring the area, trying to find her. I would follow you, in a state of shock, as desperate as you, or even more. But I knew exactly what happened.

The police, for lack of any other lead, concluded that Jade had probably been kidnapped. But she was never kidnapped. She died. And her body is still there . . .

Sarah, Alexis, Rollin, I saw everything.

Yes, everything.

I knew where Jade was, but I didn't say a word.

Don't think badly of me. The reason I later climbed for years, risking my life on dangerous rock faces, and the reason I sought refuge in writing, was only to bear my share of the burden, to confront the situation more fairly, and to offer fate a chance to strike me down. Success has never gone to my head. My head, since that day in August 2001, has been too full of the secrets I could not share . . . I had to wall myself off in silence if I wanted to save my skin. Today, I owe you the truth.

I have entrusted the events of that terrible day to a manuscript. Everything that happened you will find in its pages. I am not playing games with you: I didn't know what else to do. Being a writer is life and my death sentence. The manuscript is locked in a safe-deposit box in my name at the Geneva branch of HSBC. With that manuscript there is also a sum of money, which Sarah will be able to share between the three of you, if necessary, to rebuild a future somewhere else. I have often envisioned disappearing, wiping myself out. In case the past caught up with me. That's what some criminals do, isn't it, when the past catches up with them? With Jade dead, how could I fully enjoy a success that I had built on a series of tragedies?

Nevertheless, I did so. Until today.

The reason I am addressing the three of you is because we lived through the tragedy of Jade together. Because it tore something from all of us. And because now, when I am no longer facing your judgment, the truth can be told.

Marceau

I sit for a long time without moving, unable to let go of the letter. The whisky is now making me feel nauseous. Goddamn it, Marceau, what are you trying to tell us? What is this damned manuscript? How could I live by your side all these years without realizing anything? Jade disappeared, end of story—it can't be any other way. It was my idea for the five of us to go trekking to celebrate our twentieth birthdays. If I hadn't suggested that stupid hike, none of this would have happened, and you would still be by my side or in your study. My hands are shaking, and everything is jumbled in my head. I'm afraid of what I'm going to discover, what *we* are going to discover. So, all your mysteries were merely a foreshadowing of an even bigger storm, whose consequences I already dread. Unconsciously, I felt the first stirrings of trouble whenever you isolated yourself in your study for hours and then returned without warning. The children would rush out of their rooms to look for the attention you could no longer give them—no longer give *us* . . .

I start to panic and fling the letter onto the floor. But I need more than that to steady my nerves. I need something in my hand, anything, immediately, and I need that thing to break, to hurt, and to disappear from my sight. I grab the whisky bottle by the neck and hurl it across the living room, aiming at the view of the mountains in the windows. The glass shatters, and the bottle floats through the electric air before landing on the lawn. Is it wrong to hate the entire world when everything is suddenly slipping away beneath your feet and all that remains is a carpet of lies?

9

TUESDAY, JUNE 1, 2021

TWO WEEKS AFTER MARCEAU'S DEATH

The manuscript. I absolutely have to find it. I drop everything and grab the keys from the cabinet in the hall: the keys to Marceau's pickup. On the way out, I take my sweatshirt from the hook. I'm sure the bank manager will be pleased to see me dressed like this. I'm in such a hurry I don't even lock the front door. I'm pretty sure that whatever awaits me in the safety-deposit box won't be good. My whole body is tingling as if ants are crawling all over my skin. I dial Alexis's number and get his voicemail. Damn it, Alexis always replies! I try to reach Rollin, but he's unavailable too—no surprise in his case. He's always either lost his phone or forgotten to charge it. Today his forgetfulness is not amusing.

My office is on the way to Geneva, so I'll stop to let Karen know I'll be gone for the day. I've been a terrible partner these last two weeks, and the last thing I need is for Karen to get angry, but she's going to have to cancel all my appointments again today. Reynaud will have to wait for his Merry Fisher to be serviced—at least he'll understand—and two other boats in the workshop need gelcoat and new mooring ropes.

I've always been able to count on Karen, and that's been even truer since Marceau died. I can't see myself keeping anything I discover about Marceau from her, but Rollin may have already told her. Right now, unless he's also on the way to Geneva, his food truck is probably outside the Vinorama in Rivaz, below the terraced vineyards of Lavaux . . . There are always crowds of people on that side of the lake, especially now that it's a UNESCO World Heritage site. He's probably put out his board with the day's menu on it. Salads and locally sourced food with a nice white wine from the region. And if the customer is generous, he'll suggest a wine from Epesses, at seventy-five euros a bottle. But if he's opened Marceau's letter, I'm sure it's the only thing he can think about. He probably can't even hear the little train winding between the grape vines carrying its flood of tourists. How did he react when he read the letter? All those memories must be coming back to the surface for him too. And besides, it's not every day a bank contacts him about anything other than overdraft charges!

At last, I get the pickup started. I pass the hangar where Marceau stores his Savage Bobber. It'll never fly again. It's the same model as the one Marceau's father had, the plane he crashed in and died. I can't stop thinking. What's waiting for me in Switzerland? And where are Alexis and Rollin?

Once I get on the paved road, I gather speed and turn onto the D25. Visibility is better here, although it's higher up and farther from the lake. Houses flash past, and through the foliage there are intermittent glimpses of the lake sparkling in the sun. The mountain ridges of Switzerland appear on the horizon as I head for the agency. The lake and the mountains remind me that I'm living in a paradise I never wanted to leave, a paradise Marceau and I chose to live in together.

I'm suddenly jolted out of my seat. I was driving too fast and didn't see the speed bump. Maybe I'd best not spend too long at the agency. I don't know how long I'll be stuck at the bank in Geneva, and I absolutely have to be back by the time the children get in from school. They're twelve and ten and, in normal circumstances, are usually perfectly capable of coping. But for the past two weeks, they've been left too much to their own devices. Everything's upside down; nothing's the way it was. I've never been good at organizing things, but now I've really let things go. The house hasn't been tidied, the refrigerator is empty, and the dirty washing is piling up. This morning, I lost my temper and yelled at them. Benjamin left without kissing me, and Hermione told me I was a bad mother. So I certainly wouldn't want them to see the mess I left. I didn't pick up the shards of glass from the living room floor, nor did I recover the half-empty bottle of whisky from the garden. Since Marceau died, I've had the feeling I'm floating. The drugs the doctor prescribed and the lack of sleep don't help.

I pass luxurious properties with huge gardens that lead straight down to the lake. I know them by heart, having passed them every day. Not that I would ever want to swap my house for one of these sterile, soulless high-tech villas. They're easier to see from the lake, and I get an eyeful of them whenever I use the speedboat to get to the agency. Occasionally, when I'm jogging and I move away from the path along the shore, I venture to the edges of the private gardens and even sometimes go in when the gate is open and there's no risk of some huge watchdog attacking me. That's how, one day, I saved one of the owners. The old lady was lying on her neatly tended English lawn beneath her rosebushes, which were dancing in the wind as if laughing at her and saying, "No clippers today!" As I leaned over her, I hesitated for a moment about whether I should help her. I recognized her. She had almost sunk the agency after complaining to the mayor about our boats.

"They deface the landscape," she had said, brandishing various laws about protecting the lake. Now, she was looking at me with panic in her eyes. I was dripping with sweat, my face flushed from jogging. I considered throwing all her legal arguments back at her, but then the desperate look in her eyes got the better of me. I took my cell phone from my armband and called an ambulance. I could see that she'd sensed my hesitation, and I knew after that she would never dare cross paths with Karen and me again. From then on, she'd leave us alone.

My fingers are restless on the wheel. I see three guys staggering out of a bar. They turn as I drive past them, and I recognize one of them as the manager at Lake Pleasure Boats, our biggest competitor. It's not yet noon, and he's already hammered. I almost manage to smile at him when he waves at me with that smug air of his. I have to remember to tell Karen that his chance to buy the *Cap Camarat*, which I've spruced up, is only good until Friday. Other buyers are interested. If he doesn't make an offer soon, he'll miss his chance.

I park the pickup outside the agency. A slight breeze is blowing over the lake, the flags of the boats—French, Swiss, and Italian—float in the air, and loose halyards flap against the masts. For a moment I sit there before I switch off the engine. I can't avoid seeing my face in the rear-view mirror. My complexion is gray, there are lines everywhere, and I haven't even brushed my hair. How can I have let myself go like this? I spot Karen on the dock. She can see me, I'm sure of it; she can see how disheveled I look. I give her the usual wave. It's a ritual between us, which means, *Take it easy.* Without skipping a beat, she responds with the same signal, but I know she isn't fooled. She's doing what she can, and so am I. She's just finishing with a customer. They're inspecting a speedboat, one of our new models. Checklist before departure, final instructions, handing over the keys and the navigation kit. Mechanically, I count the number of available boats moored at the landing stage. There are seven of them, including two of our most expensive models.

A customer is walking up and down the office reception area, a coffee in his hand. I recognize him from the felt hat he wears. He likes Kazaar, the most intense flavor in the Nespresso range. The midnight-blue capsules. He settles down on the couch, facing the bay window that looks out to the lake. The view is stunning, and customers love it. Karen and I wanted to make this reception area a pleasant, relaxing place. She chose the decor. She has innate good taste. The south-facing space swims in amazing light. A Swiss designer conceived of the furniture and had it custom made by a local craftsman with spruce from the surrounding forests. Adjustable blinds in stained wood soften the light when the sun is too strong. And when the winters aren't too harsh, the sun is sometimes enough to heat the agency.

Karen has finished with her customer and comes to meet me. She walks slowly along the dock, elegant and as flawless as her outfit: spotlessly white sneakers, perfectly cut pants in natural linen that leave her ankles bare, a gray-and-pink-striped sweatshirt. I feel wretched in my grimy jeans and soiled sneakers. She gives me a concerned look, and I lose whatever composure I have left. I know I look like shit. She puts her arms around me, a gesture of affection we haven't shared in a long time, probably because work has been so busy. I can't hold back my tears. Karen hugs me tighter. There's nothing to say. I forget all about my intention to tell her about Marceau's letter.

"Sarah, I can manage here," she whispers in my ear. "You need to take care of yourself. Stay home with the kids—they need you. You can come back to work when you're ready."

I breathe a thin "Yes."

She continues to look at me. Everything is cracking inside me, but I don't say anything more.

"Just note the priorities on the calendar, Sarah, and I'll take care of them. I'm sorry, I have to go. Someone's getting impatient."

The man with the hat is waiting for her on the dock. He's a loyal customer—best not to upset him. I don't know how Karen manages to juggle everything. She can't count on her husband, Rollin, who's always gallivanting around in his food truck. She's got their daughter, Zoé, her homework, her extracurricular activities, the upkeep of the house, the work at the agency—and God knows there's plenty of that. Somehow, she manages it all and even finds time to dress nicely. Basically, she could keep the business running on her own, which scares me a bit. I've never really succeeded at balancing work and family. Maybe that's why Hermione calls me a "bad mother" and Benjamin is so elusive. I used to focus mostly on work, and maybe that's one of the reasons the distance between Marceau and me gradually started to grow. Maybe he was already moving away from me before his accident. Terrible images flash in in my mind: his dislocated body, the blood on his face.

PART TWO:
CHASING SHADOWS

10

KAREN

I hear the engine of the truck start up again. It isn't Sarah I imagine at the wheel, but Marceau. He loved that old thing with its tireless engine and battered bodywork. Hearing its muffled purr hits me like a stomach punch. I look up and see Sarah through the windshield, her sunglasses on. Not that it's a particularly sunny day, but that's Sarah. She prefers to be blind. I'm not judging. It's how she is: She runs on instinct.

Suffering is magnetic. It prowls around, then plants its invisible electrodes in your flesh and sends shocks through you. Sarah knows I understand her grief, but she doesn't imagine quite how much. She's not the only one who's suffering. I'm just better at concealing it. For how much longer? I can't unburden myself to her, or to anyone, for that matter. I would totally lose control. *She* has a right to explode; I don't. She's his wife, his widow.

Witnessing her pain, day after day, is hard, and it doesn't seem like she's reached rock bottom yet. When she's finally completely bogged down by craziness, she'll take foolish risks. That's what she does. It's her signature, her strength and her weakness—it's unavoidable. And that freaks me out because I know I'll pay the price, one way or another.

But she'll rise to the surface again. She always does. Sarah is a wild animal with a built-in survival instinct. I sensed that from the first day we met. An untamable strength, unstable and expansive, courses through her veins. Today, there's a ball of rage hardening inside her. I feel it. I see it in her face—and that's not a good omen.

There are all kinds of things I remember. Like the day we took the tug out to tow one of our boats that had broken down on the lake. The customer was a nice man, but he'd carelessly ignored the rules of navigation and collided with another boat. Sarah leaped onto the boat in distress, grabbed the rope the customer had laboriously tied to the boat he'd just rammed, and yanked on it so hard she tore the cleat from the deck. I'll never forget the fury in her eyes. They'd turned from blue to gray, as gray as the lake when a storm is threatening.

That's the strength of our duo, the way we complement each other. She's capable of machinations that are beyond me—sometimes, they're indispensable in a business like ours. With her, I always knew things would work out. Her confidence, her determination to see our project through. The promise of a bright future. I surround myself with capable people, and as long as the business is doing well, I'm fine. I've learned to defend my territory and take what I need from other people if I must. Always within the bounds of the law, or at least almost always. I'm not as clean as I may seem. But who is clean?

Part of the reason I'm making it a point of honor right now to mitigate Sarah's inadequacies is because it gives me a chance not to think so much about the fact that Marceau is dead. Without him, Sarah will never be the same. And I'll be different too. Rollin has already changed. He's distant, distracted, gets irritable more easily. As for Zoé, Marceau's death has given her nightmares. When you're nine years old, death is too sudden, shocking. I wish I could tell her how Marceau was radiant and mysterious at the same time—how he *really* was. I can't. Zoé smiles when I open the door to her room, she shows me her lovely drawings, but the music she plays on a loop betrays her anxieties.

I've always been good at sensing the emotions of those around me, even the best concealed. I can't explain it; it's something I inherited from my mother. The blows she endured from my father made her acutely aware of the slightest twitch of an eyebrow, the smallest change of mood. Until the day she hit him back and walked out, taking me with her as her only baggage. I learned from what I saw and heard, even when I pressed my hands over my ears. I didn't make the same mistakes as my mother.

What Sarah is feeling now suggests there's worse to come. It must be said that Marceau took quite a few secrets with him to the grave. And I hope they're gone for good.

My phone vibrates in my pocket. A text.

I just got in. Where's Dad?

Rollin should be at home. I don't like leaving Zoé on her own, and he knows that. She's still too young.

He won't be long, have your snack.

I call Rollin and get his voicemail. I hang up, then try again before leaving a message. I drum on the desk with my fingers. I reply casually to a female customer who comes in, handing her a brochure listing the services of the agency. While she looks through the first few pages, I text Rollin. He's always so distracted. I hope at least he has his phone with him. I get a notification that the message has been delivered but not read.

What the hell is he doing? If he isn't with Zoé within the hour, I'm going to be pissed. We're not on the same page when it comes to parenting Zoé, which is the source of a lot of arguments. He likes to be "cool dad" and not have too many boundaries. If he had his way, Zoé would be left to her own devices, whereas I watch over her. The day I found Zoé with her hair stinking of cigarettes when he was supposed to be looking after her, I threw him out of the house and made him sleep in his food truck. The next day, she was still complaining of a sore throat. I've had it with Rollin's concept of freedom without restraint, and I'm tired of his lack of ambition. I need to dream big. Marceau had big dreams, even though there were times when his silence was unbearable.

Sarah and I had known each other for a while before she talked to me about Marceau's dark side. She shouldn't have. She doesn't know it, but I didn't see Marceau the same way after that. I even talked to him differently. I knew I was getting into a gray area, but it didn't stop me. I kept fishing at the right moments for more insights from Sarah about Marceau. Not at the office, but sometimes when we took a boat out on the lake, there would be a moment's silence after we'd left the dock, and then she'd feel free to talk. As if being far from the shore, with the water lapping against the hull, gave her permission to relax. The same thing would happen in the mountains. On a hike, under the trees, lost in the vegetation, she's different. That's what drew Marceau to her, he told me one day. It's her unique connection with nature that makes Sarah so elusive, so indefinable. Once, Marceau even told me straight out that she'd probably end up leaving him. I'm sure he never imagined he'd be the first to go, as early as that, as suddenly as that. He sometimes wondered if the children were reason enough for Sarah to stay, aware that this safeguard would disappear as they grew up. That's why he distanced himself more and more from Sarah—almost imperceptibly, but in a very real way. So it wouldn't be too much of a blow when the time came. And yet he loved her. And she loved him.

Marceau also confided in me when we found ourselves out on the lake, far from the shore, on the little speedboat he and Sarah kept moored at their dock at the bottom of their garden. One day, before putting on his diving mask and taking the regulator between his teeth, he said something that still haunts me:

"It's dangerous to plunge back into the past. If you get too close to it, you can never get rid of it."

We always feel guilty about tragedies we could have avoided.

And then, as he did each time, he would drop backward off the boat like a frogman. I would find myself alone on board, watching Marceau's flippers sink into the depths of the crystalline water. I would set my stopwatch for forty-five minutes. Forty-five minutes during which Marceau would go down to his father's plane, more than a hundred feet beneath the surface.

I never knew Marceau's father or his sister, Jade. I was an honorary member of the gang. Their history wasn't mine. Unlike Sarah, Rollin, and Alexis, I hadn't experienced those tragedies firsthand. As the minutes ticked by, the bubbles would disappear from the surface of the water. He was somewhere down below, in his world of shadows and tragedy. I was the only one who could accompany him; he had chosen me for that. Personally, I've always avoided deliberately confronting things that haunt me, and the part of him that kept returning to the plane scared me as much as it attracted me. He never told me what he did at the bottom of the lake. These trips were meant to stay strictly between us. Sarah may have suspected something, but she never mentioned it. He always dove with a box of equipment. I imagined him maintaining the wreck of the plane, freeing it of plankton and seaweed, maybe even sitting on the bottom of the lake near the plane to meditate in silence and solitude. I never tried to find out more, for fear of breaking the spell. And anyway, imagination has always been more important to me than facts. He would always come back up after forty-five minutes, the bubbles announcing his reemergence. Had he found what he was looking for? Had he left at the bottom of the lake the unbearable suffering I could see in his eyes? When he returned from his solitary journeys, he was silent. His eyes were misty, his gaze distant, his mind elsewhere. He reminded me of a lost child or someone with PTSD. He would let me drive the boat back to shore.

Whenever I saw Marceau being interviewed on TV, and the interviewer would ask him the inevitable question "Where do you get your inspiration, Marceau Miller?" he would always pause for two or three seconds before answering. After a while, the silences grew longer. The critics seized on this, seeing it as a sign of his vanity, saying he was overdoing it, striking a pose. But I knew it wasn't a pose. At such moments, as in those when he managed to say a few words to me about Jade, his face would assume the faraway look he had when he came back up from his dives. It was as if the mask he habitually wore in public had fallen off. The fact was, he did lie to interviewers—not without talent, I have to admit. He did it with humor and wit, but he lied. If, paradoxically, he projected a disarming image of sincerity, *it's because part was always true.* There was something terrifying about the mystery he protected so well, the mystery that was the muse of his writing and perhaps the most private thing he possessed.

Every time a new novel of his came out, Sarah, Rollin, Alexis, and I were in the habit, like a ritual, of watching him on the top literary show on TV. Rollin and Alexis would behave like little kids, ready to laugh at his every joke. Only Sarah and I were capable of interpreting Marceau's almost imperceptible moments of distress. *Interpreting* may be an exaggeration because neither of us would have been able to say what we really meant. What's for sure is that we cared about him, and those lapses worried us.

Today, I can hardly breathe. I will never again see the bubbles coming back to the surface. He has gone from my life. I tear out pages from my diary where I've marked the dates of our upcoming appointments, which now will never come. Dates where the word *Manureva* appears, the name he gave our excursions. They were our way of escaping—it hardly mattered where we went. I didn't know at first that *Manureva* was the name Alain Colas gave his boat. Alain Colas was a sailor who disappeared in 1978 in a cyclone off the Azores. His body was never found. The last anyone heard of him was his final desperate *Mayday, mayday, mayday.* With hindsight, I find the fact that Marceau chose that name to be darkly ironic.

I mark out with a black ballpoint pen the *Manureva* scheduled for the coming week. I mark it so hard the line appears, like a scar, on the pages for the following two weeks. Come to think of it, *Manureva* was almost prophetic. It's the name of a boat with a curse on it, and its captain fell victim to that curse.

11

My emotions are a mess, and I can't untangle them. I'm angry with myself for cracking up in front of Karen. Our complicity, that silent connection we've always had, suddenly seems tainted with a hint of something murky. In the past, all it took was one look and we understood each other. Today, I recognized shadows that I don't want to see.

Karen's pain at the loss of Marceau—yes, she's hurting too—was almost tangible. Her determination to hold back her tears, I would never have suspected. The things I confided to her in the past, my doubts about Marceau, come back to me like so many possibilities of betrayal. Those moments they shared, those excursions on the lake that I pretended to know nothing about, take on a new dimension. The image of Marceau and Karen on our speedboat. It's like my best friend has stolen part of my husband.

I think again about Marceau, his need for space, his dives down to the wreck of his father's plane. That secret garden that I respected, out of love, has now become the breeding ground for doubts. The idea that Karen may have been able to share part of him that was inaccessible to me twists my stomach.

Gradually, an insidious question worms its way into me. What if Marceau confided in Karen things he never told me? This thought, both seductive and terrifying, leaves me torn between the desire to know more and the fear of what I might discover.

Lost in thought, I almost miss the turnoff to Thonon Road, which will take me to Geneva, and I give the wheel a violent jerk. The landscape flashes by, still dominated in the distance by the mountains and their white peaks and the blue of the lake. I try to collect my thoughts. Only Marceau Miller would imagine a script like this. Who else would anticipate his own death at the age of forty? Who else would leave a manuscript in a safety-deposit box in Switzerland? Marceau always liked playing games, but I can't imagine him manipulating our feelings just for the hell of it. In his letter, Marceau also mentioned money. Where does this money come from? I never noticed money being transferred from our account to another. I knew approximately how much Marceau earned in royalties, at least I thought I did, and he kept me informed about his investments. I feel overwhelmed, and all I want is to collect what's there and rush home to read the manuscript.

It's strange. When Marceau was alive, I never read his novels before they were published for fear of undermining him with my comments. After a while he stopped asking me for my opinion. I think that hurt him. When it came to other people's emotions, Marceau was a sponge. In fact, that's where his talent lay, how he created his characters. When it comes down to it, I'm probably the one responsible for the distance that developed between us without even being aware of it.

I cross the border into Switzerland. I see the huge fountain on the lake. Nearly five hundred feet high, it's the emblem of Geneva, photographed by all the tourists on their smartphones from the Quai du Général-Guisan.

The noise of a car horn makes me jump. I slam on the brakes. My pickup has come to a halt about eight inches from the bumper of a luxury sedan. A tinted window is lowered. I give him a blank look. He raises a hand clad in a leather glove, closes his window again resignedly, and goes on his way. My brain is exhausted from sleepless nights, and my reflexes are slow.

Parked outside HSBC, I see Alexis's red Porsche. I don't know anything about sports cars, but this one I recognize. A 1984 Targa. I'm surprised Alexis hasn't bothered to have the dent on the front bumper repaired, especially since he cares a lot about appearances. Marceau loved driving the car, though Alexis let him take the wheel reluctantly. He wasn't wrong—it was Marceau who left the dent.

Alexis was the leader of the gang. After high school, he studied at a business college before joining a multinational corporation, where he "dabbles in business," as he likes to put it. Always dressed impeccably—made to measure suits, Berluti shoes—he spends most of his time on planes, jetting from one meeting to another all over Europe. Right now, he's getting on my nerves. But everything is getting on my nerves. He could at least have told me he was coming here today. I'm Marceau's wife, damn it. *His widow.*

I park half on, half off the sidewalk, grab my bag, and climb out of the pickup, untangling myself from the seat belt. To hell with the parking meter. If I have to pay a fine, I might as well go all the way. I cross the street without glancing at the traffic, provoking a cascade of horns. I can't take my eyes off the gleaming Porsche parked just opposite, which just screams, *Look at me, I'm a success!* Reaching it, I look through the front window. On the passenger seat, I see Rollin's cap. Is he here too? They haven't wasted any time, those two! What do they think? That the bank manager's going to open the safety-deposit box without waiting for me? I'm the only one who's entitled to collect whatever's in it! I plan to be the first to read the manuscript! I walk into the bank, ignoring the doorman. If he as much as opens his mouth, I'll let him have it. Him and everyone else.

~

Alexis and Rollin are sitting on one of the leather couches in the lobby. They're as pale as I'm bright red. Rollin is nervously hammering the floor with his right foot. Seeing me, Alexis places a hand on Rollin's knee to calm him. He's wearing the same suit as the manager, who now comes toward us. The man makes a small gesture of greeting with his hand, at the same time glancing up at the security camera, then without further ado, asks us to follow him. I don't even have time to ask Alexis and Rollin why they didn't call me before coming. As if understanding why I'm so annoyed, Rollin attempts to justify their actions—as awkwardly as ever.

"Karen told me you were on your way. Alexis was near Rivaz, so he came and picked me up. Rolling up here in my food truck wasn't the best option. Basically, I just dumped everything outside the Vinorama."

"We've put a room aside for you to open the box," the manager cuts in, apparently in a hurry to get this over with.

With the boys behind me, I follow the manager to the elevators. We ride down to the lower basement and walk along a corridor until we come to a reinforced door. The manager nods to the security guard who's standing there, and we're admitted to the strong room. For me, this is a first.

The box is on a table in the middle of the room. Everything is very cold and very sterile. The size of the box surprises me—much bigger than I've always imagined these things to be. I hesitate for a moment before approaching the table. Rollin and Alexis stay back. The manager points them to some armchairs at the other end of the room. My hands are shaking; I don't know what to do. The manager whispers the electronic code for the box, then leaves the room. I immediately type the code, and there's a metal click, and the box opens. Inside, there's a bag. Nothing else. I pull it toward me. It's heavy. Alexis and Rollin haven't taken their eyes off me. I try to ignore them as I open the zipper.

I can't believe it.

The bag is full of money. Where does all this cash come from? Did Édouard pay him in cash, or what? Anxiously, I plunge my hands deep inside the bag. All I'm interested in is the manuscript. I turn the banknotes over, digging deeper and deeper.

"Are you all right, Sarah?" Alexis asks.

I don't reply. I tip the bag upside down and shake it with all my might. The banknotes whirl about above the table and scatter at my feet. I start screaming like a madwoman.

"*Where's the manuscript?*"

My anger mixes with my tears. Alexis and Rollin look at each other, bewildered. They're even paler than they were when I arrived. Being the kind of person he is, Alexis nevertheless manages to preserve his stoical air, while Rollin buries his head in his hands and sobs. All our memories come back to the surface. Jade. A foul mess. Fear, questions without answers. In a fraction of a second, the same pain—the same dread—seizes all three of us. The tsunami that has swept over my brain stops me from seeing clearly, and yet, in this maelstrom, I sense that something isn't right. My muscles tightening, my breath coming in short gasps, I start moving around the table like a fury, tramping on the dozens and dozens of banknotes scattered across the floor. Alexis is so nervous he's biting his nails as he stares at the bag. Rollin nods his head like a boxer who's just taken a right hook in the face. Too many tragedies, too many things unsaid, too much money.

Too many coincidences.

As if something has clicked inside me, I wind the movie backward at high speed and say, "He didn't fall."

Rollin emerges abruptly from his trance and stares at me aghast.

Alexis has already stood up. He looks at me with his hard, penetrating gaze. "What are you talking about?"

"He was murdered. Somebody murdered Marceau."

12

Alexis places a hand firmly on my shoulder. I can't help detecting in this gesture a barely contained aggressiveness. He's always thought I'm crazy, I know. But this weak attempt at asserting his authority isn't going to scare me.

"You're way off track, Sarah. He fell, something we all dreaded would happen. He knew the risks he was taking; he even told us in his letter."

"No! It was no accident. I'm sure of it. Somebody killed Marceau."

"Sarah, the police who were on the scene were clear about it. If they'd had the slightest doubt, if they'd noticed anything suspicious, they'd have launched an investigation."

I break free of him. I'm not giving up. "If anyone, you two have to believe me at least!"

"Sarah, we all wish this had never happened. You weren't the only one who told him to stop. It was a terrible accident, but it's not surprising. You're in shock, and that's only natural. But you must be strong, for the sake of Benjamin and Hermione."

I turn to Rollin, dripping with sweat, his face red. It looks like he's totally losing it.

"Rollin, say something, damn it!" Alexis cries, and then, "That's enough, Sarah! We're all on edge, and . . . and of course it reminds us of what we lived through twenty years ago."

Then, turning to Rollin, he said, "Are you going to tell her or not? Tell her it was an accident!"

Lips quivering, Rollin mutters a few words, so quietly we can barely hear him. "The . . . the police . . . It was an accident, Sarah."

I hurl the bag against the wall.

"And what about the manuscript? Where's the fucking manuscript?"

Alerted by the noise, the manager knocks at the door, half opens it, and warily puts his head into the gap. The security guard is behind him, ready to intervene.

"Is everything all right?" he asks.

"Yes, everything's fine," Alexis replies. To keep up appearances, he takes me in his arms and runs his hand through my hair, the way you'd stroke a frightened dog. "She's upset. I'm sure you can understand . . ."

Reassured, the manager withdraws, closing the door behind him. I immediately break free of Alexis. I've never felt so angry. No, nothing's fine! Rollin has sat down in his armchair, looking like he's about to pass out. He and Alexis both look terrified, each in his own way, and I'm afraid too, but what terrifies me the most is that they don't believe me. Even worse, my best friends are telling me I'm crazy. I head for the door, trampling the money scattered on the floor, brushing past them.

"It's anything but an accident," I say again.

The security guard moves aside as I pass. As I walk toward the elevator, I can hear the manager and Alexis talking in low voices. I can only make out a few words.

". . . first time . . . scene like this . . ."

The idiot! I cross the lobby and walk through the revolving door.

I have an idea, and nothing is going to change my mind. I have to find that manuscript.

As I pass Alexis's Porsche, I kick the car door as hard as I can, making a small dent in it. Not a big one, but big enough to make me feel better. By some miracle, my pickup hasn't been towed away, and there's no ticket on the windshield. I see my reflection in the window on the driver's side. My hair is disheveled, and my eyes are bloodshot. There's a red blotch on my face, another on my neck.

I have two hours to get back to Yvoire, take a shower, and be presentable when the kids get home from school. They've been shaken enough. I don't want to upset them even more. Benjamin worries me: He's been stammering since Marceau died. It was a big shock to him. I even thought I might take him to see a child psychiatrist, but I couldn't summon up the energy. It may also be that I don't want to be questioned by the shrink, who would surely be as interested in me as in Benjamin.

I've been driving for a while before I look in my bag for my cell phone. I wedge it on the dashboard so that I can keep one eye on the screen. It's vibrated several times since I left Geneva. Three texts from Alexis, sent at intervals of less than five minutes.

> Sarah, I'm so sorry. We're all on edge. I'm here if you need me. And I'm not angry about the door, even though it squeaks a little when I open it now.

> Sarah, try to get some rest. We'll find the manuscript.

> Sarah, it's me again. The manager counted the money. Marceau left $3,175,000.

The money, that's all he cares about. Having said that, Marceau's letter has clearly rattled him. As for Rollin, he's lost it completely. I scratch my neck, making the unsightly red blotch even worse. Luckily, the one on my face is fading.

Leaving Douvaine, I decide to continue straight on to Thonon-les-Bains instead of turning off in the direction of Yvoire. The engine sputters as I accelerate. The needle of the gauge is close to STOP. The bottom of the old tank is full of impurities the carburetor can't quite handle. I pass a service station without stopping. Too bad about the tank, but I have one objective, which is to tell the police everything: Marceau's letter, the manuscript, the money, and especially my doubts about the accident. I can hear my breath getting quicker and feel my face twitching. The pickup drifts slightly, the tires screeching against the sidewalk. At the last moment, I manage to get back on course. A car coming toward me flashes its headlights. In response, I hoot my horn several times. I feel like screaming. Why won't they just leave me alone?

What happened, Marceau? Until I get answers to my questions, I won't stop. I need to know where all this leads.

When I get to the police station in Thonon, I park in a reserved spot, the only one available. I rush past the desk sergeant and head straight for Delmas's office.

"Madame, you're not allowed!" an officer calls after me. A moment or two later, he grabs me by the shoulder.

But Delmas has seen me coming.

"I'll deal with it," he says.

The officer lets go of me.

"You can't just come bursting in here, Madame Miller. Let's go into my office."

Delmas gives his colleague a sympathetic look and motions me to follow him.

"I know what you must be going through, Madame Miller," he says before we've even sat down.

"No, you don't."

I feel as if I'm plugged into an electric socket. It's impossible to calm down. Why do I get the impression everyone's against me? I sit down and fumble in my bag for a handkerchief.

"So, Madame Miller," Delmas resumes in a sickly sweet voice, "tell me what brings you here."

His constant repetition of *Madame Miller* is getting on my nerves, and I'm losing my patience with how he's talking down to me. I twist my handkerchief until it's just shreds in my hands.

"Marceau sent me a letter . . ."

Delmas looks at me anxiously. "I think what you mean, Madame Miller, is that you found a letter, right?"

I bring my hands down hard on his desk. Delmas looks me up and down, which only increases my anger. Does he also think I'm crazy?

"I received a letter from HSBC this morning, *Monsieur Delmas*, together with a letter from Marceau that the bank was supposed to let me have if my husband died. Rollin Uldry and Alexis Thorens also received copies. In it, Marceau mentions a manuscript containing new information about the disappearance of his sister, Jade, twenty years ago."

Delmas's eyes grow larger, as if he's just seen a ghost. "Can I see that letter, Madame Miller?"

"Of course. That's why I'm here."

As I put it down on his desk, his eyes move back and forth from the letter to my face. He carefully unfolds the sheets of paper.

"These dark marks on the paper are blood. Can you explain what it's doing there, Madame Miller?"

"It's nothing. I cut myself opening the envelope."

I'm certainly not going to mention the episode of the bookcase and the bottle of Dalmore. His eyes linger on me for a moment as if he doesn't believe me.

He takes his time reading the letter, occasionally breaking off to stare insistently at me.

"And did you collect the money and the manuscript?" he asks when he's finished.

"Only the money. Three million dollars in cash, loose bills in a duffel bag, but there was nothing else in the safety-deposit box."

"Three million . . ." Delmas frowns and pauses to think. When he resumes speaking, it's slowly and as if he's weighing every word. "It's possible your husband never put the manuscript in that box. After all, his letter isn't dated. It may be quite old. Or maybe he never finished writing it? I imagine that must happen to writers. Not being sufficiently satisfied with their work, constantly revising. No, as far as I'm concerned, it's the money that puzzles me. Nobody puts so much cash aside for no reason . . ."

He stops for a moment and scratches his head, as if embarrassed to share what he's about to say next.

"In his letter, he talks about disappearing. What is he referring to? And why did he also send this letter to your two friends?"

I stand up and lean on the desk. The scent he's wearing, a strong fragrance of leather and spices, is making me nauseous. It's much too manly for this short, thin, unattractive guy. Everything about him repels me, but I have to keep my cool.

"Let's talk about that. When I saw that money, I immediately thought that Marceau didn't fall off that damned rock face all by himself. Someone must have pushed him. And the manuscript hasn't vanished for no reason. My husband never talked to me about his work, and I only read his books when they were published. So, if he mentions this manuscript so clearly in his letter, it's because it exists. And it's finished. Marceau also states that Jade didn't disappear, contrary to the conclusion of the investigation at the time. Something happened twenty years ago that we don't know about, and he wanted to tell us."

I sit down again, suddenly exhausted.

"Why not earlier?" I say, almost to myself. "Why he didn't talk about it, I don't know."

For a moment, I'm lost in my thoughts. Then I force myself to continue.

"But if this manuscript is nowhere to be found, Captain Delmas, it's for a good reason. Marceau was killed deliberately . . ."

He hasn't taken his eyes off me. "You're getting a bit ahead of yourself, Madame Miller. Your husband went climbing without safety equipment. He knew the risks. He even mentions that in his letter. As far as the manuscript is concerned, maybe you should look in his study, check his computer, memory sticks, hard drives, all that kind of thing. If it's there, you'll find it, and if you do, come back and see me."

"Are you kidding me? What about the wound on his face? He fell on his back, so that must be a blow he received before he fell. A blow from somebody."

"Madame Miller, my men were on the scene immediately. They didn't find anything suspicious, and believe me, they scoured the whole area. As for the wound, the medical examiner ran extra tests but didn't come to any definite conclusion. As for your husband's sister, that case goes back to the days of Yves Reynaud. It's ancient history. And Reynaud is stubborn as a mule. If he'd had a lead, he would have followed it long ago. The files show that there are more than forty thousand disappearances in France each year. I'm sorry to say, but Jade's case is unfortunately an all-too-common occurrence. Your husband was a writer; he probably let his imagination run riot and invented another end to his sister's story."

Delmas must take me for an idiot. I pick up Marceau's letter and, at the same time, send a plastic jar filled with pens flying off the desk.

Delmas grabs me by the wrist. "Don't try that with me, Madame Miller. The next time you disrespect me, I'll book you for assaulting an officer. Is that understood?"

We stare at each other, but his exasperation is nothing compared to my hatred. I'll have to prove it without his or anyone else's help.

13

THE MANUSCRIPT

I hesitated for a long time before writing this story. It took me months after the events to make my mind up to write these pages. During that time, the police wound up their investigation, concluding that Jade had "disappeared." I quickly flushed down the toilet all the crap the doctors had prescribed to help me cope, the prescriptions that were messing with my head. The hardest part was over: I realized there was no point in waiting for a truth that would never come. Nobody understood what a shock I'd had. The woman shrink I consulted called me fragile and hypersensitive—what a discovery! The loss of my father ten years earlier had created a fault line in me. She had no idea how deep it went. She couldn't, since I never gave her any clue to the reason for that impossible death. In her opinion, my sister's disappearance had aggravated my depression, plunging me into a state of total inertia.

So I decided to fight on alone, against or with my demons, substituting my pen for my sessions with the shrink. I decided to write, for once, not fiction but the truth.

Is every truth worth writing down, though? How can I measure the impact of a story I could not reveal in my lifetime? This question haunts me. It may be assumed—as I do myself—that it's an escape mechanism, a way of relieving myself of a burden without fearing the judgment of others. Yet I also see it as a duty. My manuscript is a time bomb, one that will explode after my death. The truth will survive me.

I think about Sarah and the children. If there's a loose thread, I know that Sarah will pull on it. Her need to understand everything sometimes makes her uncontrollable, unpredictable. With this manuscript, I hope to give her the answers she's looking for. She will think I should have done so earlier, but I was not capable of doing so. I'm not capable of doing so. It would be too devastating. This delayed confession is one I owe to her and to our two children—and I imagine she will understand why I've acted this way. As for Alexis and Rollin, they've always been extremely loyal to me. Without their presence and support, I would have gone under long ago. The ties we've had since we were teenagers have only grown stronger. They are intimately linked to the memory of my sister, and thanks to them, that memory will never fade. True friendships are built on the trials you endure, not on the fun you share . . .

I've been writing and rewriting this manuscript for years. It's not a question for me of satisfying a writer's fantasies—in a way, what newfound freedom!—but of refining the truth a little more each time. As the years go by, and the weight of guilt grows, things appear to me in a new light.

"Writing the truth" is also my way of giving Jade her story back, including the story she wasn't able to live. My beloved sister will never know the joy of seeing her children grow. I will never see white threads appear in her hair, or lines circle her eyes. I owe her this, and besides, writing has helped me live and become the man I am. This sense of duty to confess has served as a catalyst for my emotions, previously bogged down in grief, and they have subsequently fueled my novels. An intertwined circle where reality and fiction feed on one another.

My very first novel brought me success and fame. Many people consider that an achievement, but it's an achievement that rests on private wounds, the very wounds I use to disguise the truth I'm not capable of accepting. Fear has always been a driving force for me. Fear of being abandoned, fear of being judged. The fear of a little boy who has done a really stupid thing and remains silent to delay the punishment . . .

I've delayed too long. It's time to get started.

To tell the story I have to tell, I need to begin at the beginning.

I was eight years old when we left Nice. A professional opportunity had arisen for my mother in the radiology department of the Chablais Medical Center in Thonon, Haute-Savoie. My father, whose profession allowed him to settle wherever he wished, saw new places to fly over in his plane, the famous Savage Bobber. For me, it was a great change. I could come and go as I pleased and spend most of my time outdoors, exploring the area. Given this new interest, my mother enrolled Jade and me in the Forest Center, an offshoot of the local office of tourism that offered many activities for children. It was the perfect place for the two of us. And when the accident occurred that cost my father his life, it became our refuge.

I was ten when that happened, and Jade was eleven months younger. We lived through that tragedy as children of that age live through such things. We wanted to be like all the other children, despite having one less parent. But the years passed, and the grief was still there. We were living with a ghost, hoping that when we grew up, the ghost would go away at last.

The summer I turned seventeen, the Forest Center took me on as a seasonal worker. My first summer job. Jade soon joined me in this adventure. We both became mountain guides on the most accessible and marked trails. Sarah was also a guide, and that is where we met. I immediately liked her slight Swiss accent, the sensual way she rolled her r*'s, the way she constantly reminded me that I was a French. Right from the start, Sarah's strength, her need to feel free, fascinated me. She lived for summer, for that wonderful time when she could cross the Swiss border and stay in her grandmother Louise's house—the one that became* our *house, where we raised our children. Sarah wouldn't have wanted to live anywhere else.*

It was Yves Reynaud, the policeman, who trained us as guides. He must have been about forty at the time and helped out at the center whenever he could. The old fox was a real local and knew the mountains like the back of his hand. When she was with him, Sarah would behave like a wild child, and he had a challenge trying to contain her energy. I realize now how stifled she must have felt in her parents' house in Lausanne and how free she was here.

I immediately loved working with her. Her presence became indispensable to me from the first day we spent together. There was something very special about her. She was capable of surviving in a hostile environment. The vast forests and the lake were her kingdoms. I already knew that trying to tame her would change my life forever. That's why I made an effort to hold back a little. It was the only way to avoid a fatal accident. Not that we never argued. But rather than driving us apart, every argument brought us closer together. Every time we raised our voices, we understood each other a little better. It created a common language between us. Intense as our relationship was, becoming more intimate would have changed everything at the time. We both knew the moment hadn't come yet. It would take three more years, and a tragedy, before we exchanged our first kiss. It's as if the presence of my sister was an invisible rampart between us, because it was only after her disappearance that my relationship with Sarah took a more romantic turn. I say "disappearance" because it's convenient, for the moment. The reality is quite different, and that's why I'm writing this. What happens to this manuscript won't depend on any publisher. Nor will it stay at the bottom of a drawer or a safety-deposit box in a bank. It's an airbag that's waiting for a collision in order to inflate and burst.

I've skipped a few years. So, Jade disappeared. The investigation to find her was entrusted to old Reynaud. He organized the search, going beyond the call of duty, spending day and night in the mountains he thought he knew so well. This was a man who had taught us to be humble in the face of the elements. "Remember that with every season, every change in the weather, the forests, the mountains, and even the lake change." Then, once the search came to an end, once the dogs and helicopters were gone, the case gradually slipped down the list of priorities of a discouraged police team. The case extinguished something in Reynaud. The day he retired, many years later, not only did he take away his last boxes, he dragged this deadweight with him.

I'm so sorry.

Everything should have been so different.

14

I'm out of gas. The needle on the gauge went below the little notch it mustn't pass, and the engine stopped. Now I'm walking along the side of the road, the empty gas can knocking rhythmically against my thigh. I try to keep well to the left, facing the oncoming traffic, hoping not to twist an ankle between the rough edge of the asphalt and the wild grass. It's about seven miles to Évian-les-Bains and almost as far to the Swiss border. I'm walking toward Lugrin. I remember the name of the chalet where Marceau and I often stopped when we hiked in this area. *Vapiplan*: "Hurry slowly," in the local patois. What irony!

It'll be at least a mile before I find gas, then I'll have to walk all the way back. The timing couldn't be worse, but it's my fault. Did I let this happen on purpose?

A vehicle comes up behind me in the other lane. I turn and wave, brandishing the can. The woman, in a convertible, wearing sunglasses, ignores me. No one is going to pick me up the way I look right now. On the quieter Crétal Road, there's even less of a chance that I'll come across a charitable soul. Anyway, walking helps me to take stock, think things over. The situation sums me up: abandoned at the side of the road, filthy, a pariah, forced to ask for help from people who don't want to give it to me. Sarah Miller, reduced to nothing. Empty, like her gas tank.

After about twenty minutes, not a soul in sight, I come to the service station at Lugrin. The first gas pump is out of order, but the second accepts my credit card. I unhook the nozzle and let the fuel glug into the can. The smell is overwhelming, and I've gotten it all over my hands and clothes. Leaving again, I have to shift the heavy can from one hand to the other. The smell of gas reminds me of the odor left by chainsaws used by woodcutters in the surrounding forests. I prefer the smell of freshly cut wood, the shavings flying in the air, filling the surroundings with fragrance, the smell of sap and resin, of the forest. Marceau also loved to breathe in the forest. He sometimes wrote about it in his books. Will there be at least a little of that in his manuscript?

Reaching the pickup, I fill the tank, some of it spilling down the side of the truck. But at least now I can make it to the man, maybe the only man, capable of understanding me, of understanding my distress—and my determination.

Keeping my foot on the accelerator, I devour the remaining five and a half miles, then look for the almost hidden turnoff onto a forest path. As the branches and ferns lash the truck, my wheels follow the deep track all the way down to the lake. It's here, in a renovated house nestled amid the spruce trees, that Reynaud lives. I get out of the truck, and memories are awakened in me as I run my hands over the irregular bark of a tree trunk and breathe in the lush scent of the forest. I recall a phrase by the journalist and author Christian Charrière: *"We think we are observing Nature whereas it's Nature that is looking at us, permeating us."* After a short walk, I see Reynaud sitting in his rocking chair on the front porch, a book on his knees, *The Human Stain* by Philip Roth. Reynaud seems to have dozed off, and wakes as I approach. He smiles and is the first to speak.

"I was driving that pickup before you had your license. She's relentless. But she does stink of gas. Want me to take a look at her?"

He may have gray hair, but he's as strong as an ox and still has a gleam in his eyes.

"No need, I'm the one who stinks of gas. I should have filled her up before the tank was empty . . ."

He looks at me, then gives me a big hug, and I start to cry, unable to control my sobs. This is the shoulder on which I can be myself, can let myself go.

"I miss him too," he says.

He waits for my breathing to slow down.

"I'll make you a coffee. Sit here, look at the lake, listen to it."

It's what he says when things aren't going well, and hearing his voice today is helping me feel better. I haven't been to see him since Marceau's funeral. He always knows the right words to say.

Reynaud places two cups of coffee on the table and sits down next to me.

"Do you want to talk about it, or would you prefer me to tell some of my old stories? I may have a few you haven't heard before."

I give him a tender look, a look that says, *Not today.* I prefer to get straight to the point.

"Marceau had a feeling something might happen to him, but he was prepared. Alexis, Rollin, and I received a letter."

"Strange, but it doesn't surprise me. He was a writer; he always had to have the last word."

"But this is different. He . . . he wrote something . . . about Jade. He says he owes us the truth."

Reynaud takes off his hat and turns to me. His face betrays an old, deep wound. "The truth . . . about Jade? What do you mean?"

"He put it all in a manuscript, which he was keeping in a bank. I went there. Alexis and Rollin were there when I arrived."

His breathing grows more labored. He wants to know, obviously.

"We found a sports bag, with about three million dollars, but no manuscript."

"That's not like him. He told you it'd be in the bank? Do you have the letter? I'd like to read it."

Reynaud is reacting like the police officer he used to be, like he's back on duty. The paper shakes in his hands.

"I don't think Marceau fell," I say. "I'm convinced it wasn't an accident. Someone killed him."

Reynaud looks up from the letter and stares at me—I don't completely understand the meaning of his gaze.

"Have you told the police?"

"Yes, that idiot Delmas, who looks down his nose at me. He won't do anything."

"Delmas . . . He's an opportunist, and he's vain. He always dreamed of getting rid of me. He's a coward who likes to brag about how good he is."

"He says he needs evidence to launch an investigation."

"Yes, and maybe he wants the culprit to show up and hold out his wrists to be handcuffed, preferably during station opening hours. What a loser!"

I know I can count on Reynaud. I just hope I don't get him into trouble. He stands up and walks quickly inside the house. Through the door, I hear him in his study, rummaging in his desk and in what looks like a metal chest. I peer into the main room and get a glimpse of his world. A number of gleaming shotguns hang on the wall. Fishing gear, also in perfect condition. Photographs on a sideboard, some of people I know, including one of me, Marceau, and the children. Hidden behind the pictures of the living is a photograph of Jade, a few days before she disappeared.

"Are you ready?"

I turn away as if caught in the act.

"Where are we going?"

"Where that idiot should have gone the minute you told him about your letter."

15

"I don't know what you have planned for this evening, Sarah, but our excursion is going to take a while."

"I sent Karen a text asking her to keep the children in the house."

We've been driving for some time, and the tension that's been building for days has lifted. I sink ever deeper into the passenger seat. Reynaud's determined air and the warmth inside his vehicle, sheltered from the spring wind, reassure me. I get the feeling he knows exactly what he's doing. When we get to Geneva, Reynaud finds a parking spot near the bank. As we go in, the doorman clearly recognizes me. Reynaud takes out his police ID—five years out of date—which immediately stops him from giving us any trouble. Reynaud doesn't look like someone you want to mess with.

~

"We need to ask you some questions about one of your customers."

"I can't divulge that kind of information without authorization."

"I understand . . . But this is important. You did know Marceau Miller?"

The bank clerk's face loses its professional passivity and lights up. My husband's name often has that effect.

"Ah, Marceau Miller wasn't just anybody! I loved his books. He signed copies of almost all of them for me."

Seizing the opportunity, Reynaud lightens his tone. "If you're a fan of his books, then you owe it to him to help me. It might allow us to understand the circumstances of his death."

The clerk nods, visibly moved.

"Can you tell me when Monsieur Miller came here last?"

He searches quickly on the computer in front of him.

"If it's of any help . . . Here we are. Monsieur Miller hadn't been here for a year, but he came three weeks ago, while I was on vacation . . . What a pity, I didn't get a chance to ask him to sign his last book . . . It was . . . Thursday, April twenty-second."

"Just a few weeks before he died," Reynaud says. "Could you please print that for me?"

"Of course."

"I'd also like to see the footage from your surveillance cameras. Monsieur Miller must have been captured by one of them. Who do I need to ask?"

"For that, I'd have to talk to . . ." The clerk glances quickly around. "But I might be able to save you time . . . If you'd like to follow me to the security room. They owe me a favor."

Reynaud walks ahead of me. A few hours ago, in the same building, I was so angry my blood was boiling. This time, my heart is still pounding a little, and my senses are sharpened. We're getting somewhere. We enter a dark room with modern furniture and an array of computer equipment. I'm going to see Marceau again. Marceau projected in black and white, shortly before his death.

"It's very simple," the technician says, once the manager has given his approval over the phone. "I just enter the day and hour, and we go straight to what we need. Our equipment is state of the art."

The revolving door at the entrance to the bank is motionless for a moment, and then Marceau appears. I put my hand over my mouth. Seeing him pierces my heart.

"4:44 p.m.," Reynaud notes.

"I can speed it up so we can see him come out."

"Do it," Reynaud says.

"Ah, there he is."

The technician freezes the image.

"5:04 p.m. So, he comes out again after twenty minutes, with a package under his arm."

This confirms what we had suspected. I close my eyes. A brown envelope the size of a manuscript.

Reynaud turns to the technician. "Can you print the screen captures of the entrance and exit for me?"

Once this is done, Reynaud pushes me gently toward the exit, and we get back to the car. Reynaud has an air of concentration as he adjusts his rearview mirror, and I let myself be guided by his authority.

"That's what police work is," he says. "And now, fasten your seat belt, Sarah."

Reynaud rejoins the traffic, weaving between the lanes of cars. There's much honking of horns, but he's determined to follow this lead. I don't know where we're going, and I feel slightly anxious, but I have to trust Reynaud. I'm not crazy.

The miles rush by, and the forest grows dense around us. After a while, we veer off in the direction of the mountains. I recognize the road, but this time we bypass the mountains and Lake Neuteu. I cling to the grab bar as the road gets rough. This unmarked path is the one Marceau must have taken to the rock face.

"The shock absorbers need changing," Reynaud says, "but the old girl still has it in her."

In the distance, I glimpse the remains of police tape marking off the area where Marceau's body was found. Reynaud gives me a quick glance as he turns the SUV onto a side road.

"If you want to murder a free climber, the only place to push him is from up there."

We advance along an unmarked path, the grass as tall as the windows. Suddenly, the car's undercarriage hits a rock, and the SUV is lifted off the ground. Reynaud slows down and drives another few yards, glances in the rearview mirror, and stops.

"We can't go any farther, but we're close enough," he says, unfastening his seat belt.

As I get out of the car, there's a smell of smoke. Reynaud walks back toward the rock that scraped the SUV. I join him.

"If I hit this rock, I'm sure others have as well. Nothing has changed in the last few weeks."

"What exactly are we looking for?"

"Anyone coming here with the intention of killing Marceau would also have to make sure they could get away quickly. To get ahead of Marceau in his climb, you'd need either a helicopter, which wouldn't be very discreet, or you'd have to get as close to the top as you could in a four-wheel-drive vehicle."

He looks at me as I sniff the air.

"What direction is that smell coming from, Sarah?"

"That's what I'm trying to figure out."

"Remember what I taught you."

"The direction of the wind . . . But at this altitude, and with the forest all around, I'm really not sure."

"What kind of smell is it?"

"Burned dried leaves."

"Meaning what?"

I keep trying. I don't want to disappoint him.

"Bees. Smoking out the bees. Hives!"

"Good, Sarah! Now keep thinking. Where would you put beehives in this area to guarantee their safety but still be able to gain access?"

I turn in a circle, all my senses on the alert. I listen to the forest.

"Up there! Just on the edge of the trees, before that small clearing."

He holds out his hand to me. "Let's go."

We walk up the path, cutting through the trees. After a few steps, Reynaud raises his arm and points at a truck parked a little higher up. The tailgate is wide open, and two beekeepers are taking turns removing the frames laden with honey from the hives. Reynaud motions me to stop. I see him checking the surroundings. As I come close to him, a branch cracks beneath my feet. The two beekeepers, in white clothes and masks that make them look half fencer, half NASA astronaut, turn toward us. I sense a moment's hesitation, as if they're ready to burst into a run.

"We're just tourists," Reynaud cries, raising his arms.

As we approach, the smell of smoke intensifies.

Clouds of bees, disoriented and drowsy from the smoke, start to whirl excitedly around us. I brush them away with the back of my hand.

"Don't come any closer if you don't want to be stung," one of the beekeepers calls.

One of them comes toward us, gently brushing off the insects clinging to his outfit, and lifts his mask.

"We don't want any trouble."

"This won't take long," Reynaud replies, showing his police ID. "I just have a few questions, and not about bees."

"Listen, we can work this out. We have an arrangement with a colleague of yours."

Great, they're illegally harvesting honey. I let Reynaud continue his interrogation.

"I don't care what you do. It's not what I'm here for."

"Do you want honey?"

The offer makes Reynaud smile.

"No, though I'm sure it's delicious."

"Definitely. Nobody else brings their hives up this far."

"When did you move your hives here?"

"Four or five months ago."

"Have you ever noticed any vehicles coming into the area?"

"Nobody ever comes here, that's why we chose this place. Does this have to do with the body they found two weeks ago?"

"Yes, it does."

"Everyone says the guy was climbing without a rope. You have to be really crazy to do that."

I feel my anger rising. Reynaud senses it and puts his hand on my shoulder.

"Take it easy, Sarah." Then, to the beekeeper, "Could you get your colleague over here, please? It's important."

The other man is energetically moving his bellows, creating a voluminous cloud near the hives. He breaks off and joins us.

"That accident really screwed things up for us. With all these people, we had to leave the hives unsupervised for over a week."

"But maybe you saw someone or heard something just before the accident? Or even on the same day?"

"At this time of year, I come here every two or three days. It was windy the day before the accident, and sometimes a tree branch falls and damages one of the hives, so I often do a quick check. I heard an engine like someone was patrolling in the area. I hid. It might have been a cop."

"What do you mean, you hid? Did you try to see who it was? What time was this?"

The guy shrugs. "We don't want any hassle. We prefer to keep hidden. As for the time, I remember it was around lunchtime."

"What did the engine sound like?"

"Like an engine, that's all I can tell you. Apart from the fact that whoever it was scraped the underside of whatever they were driving, just like you did. A noise like that travels."

Reynaud thanks the beekeepers.

"We still have two hours before it gets dark. I think we should try to get to the summit. We'll need to get the forensics people here to examine the rock that scraped our chassis."

He turns to me. It's the way he must have looked when he was still working. "You know it was with just a sliver of paint under the Pont de l'Alma in Paris that the experts were able to track down the Fiat Uno that hit Princess Diana's Mercedes. From that tiny piece of evidence, they were able to find the make, model, and year the car was manufactured. Even Scotland Yard was amazed. The French did a great job, and that was in 1997!"

For a few seconds, Reynaud stands there, lost in thought.

It takes us twenty minutes through thick woods to reach the summit, on the rock face Marceau was climbing. There must be some clues here. We don't need to confer with each other; we both know what we need to do. The anguish of the prolonged search for Jade twenty years ago is on our minds. Keep your fellow searcher within sight, look about you for the slightest clue—branches abnormally broken, footprints, blood, pieces of cloth—everything and anything. Peering up, down, in front of you, on either side, behind, just in case . . . The undergrowth scratches my arms. It's a grueling climb. We finally reach the summit, a ledge some sixty feet above the void.

Vertigo.

The view of the lake in the distance and the mountains is breathtaking. It's part of what Marceau would come looking for here, in addition to the adrenaline: isolation, freedom . . . alone in the world on his forbidden perch. Reynaud, still hoping there might be evidence to collect, signals to me not to walk on the sandy soil. We climb over rocks on the periphery of the overhang.

Squinting, I notice some unusual streaks on the ground. Reynaud has already seen them.

"It looks like someone tried to wipe out his tracks, probably using a branch. We'll have to collect all these broken branches. All this will need to be analyzed, and fast."

I look around. There are branches everywhere. It's going to be hell. Reynaud clearly thinks the same thing. His eyes sweep across the forest, and he frowns slightly—the first sign of discouragement he's allowed himself since we started.

~

On the way back, I feel even more tired, which is dangerous in the mountains, so I slow down. Reynaud notices, and just as I'm expecting him to put his hand on my shoulder, he curses and suddenly stops. He raises his arm and points. He's found something.

16

Reynaud's discovery gives me a burst of energy. He holds up a branch, on the end of which he's hooked a climbing sling used for carrying gear. It's been left where nobody ever comes, a place that isn't open for climbing. There's been nothing else to indicate a climber has been anywhere near here recently. Only Marceau, who was crazy about these peaks and hated rules and safety guidelines, could have ventured to this isolated rock. My doubts dissolve. This may be our first lead.

~

Darkness is falling over the forest. The light is fading fast, and the colors of the trees fade as we walk slowly back down. I'm exhausted and ready for this day to end.

Once Reynaud's at the wheel of his SUV, it's a difficult ride. We're jolted violently until the isolated path gives way to a track that's more suitable for vehicles. My phone starts to vibrate. A profusion of emails, texts, and missed calls pops up on my phone. From Karen:

> All OK with Benjamin and Hermione,
> despite the situation.

These words only half relieve me. Hermione is angry, and Benjamin is acting like his father: keeping his distance. From Alexis:

> Sarah, we need to meet, we need to talk.
> I'm worried about you.

This whole business has exploded our little circle of friends, which used to be my whole world. *Marceau, what have you started?*

Neither Reynaud nor I speak. My mind is working overtime, engulfing and destabilizing me at the same time—I feel like I'm losing control. Reynaud keeps his eyes on the road. I have no idea what he's thinking; his expression is blank, his features serious, anxious. This day has been too much for both of us.

Night settles in, and the headlights illuminate our way as we leave the main road. Reynaud slows down as we approach the forested drive to his house. The halos of the headlights illuminate nocturnal animals that disappear quickly into the trees. In the distance, the quiet sparkling of the lake is hypnotizing. Suddenly, two slivers of light appear between the high ferns and pine trees. Reynaud slams his foot on the brake, the car skidding about six feet. A deer, almost full grown, brushes against the front of the SUV, at the height of the windshield. Mechanically, Reynaud puts his arm across to protect me. My heart is pounding. The shock has startled both of us. If I'd been at the wheel, given my current state, the animal would certainly have come through the windshield. Reynaud turns to me, relieved, an almost paternal look in his eyes.

"This area is teeming with deer this time of year. I can see them from my terrace in the evening, passing like shadows in the moonlight. I could spend hours watching them drink from the lake."

I understand why he's fallen in love with this place, which is so wild and isolated. When he parks and turns off the headlights, the lake reveals itself. I gaze out at the vast, dark expanse, glittering in places, speckled by the scattered lights of boats. This colossal volume of fresh water trapped between the mountains has always exerted a magnetic force on me. I know the taste of the lake; I know its temperature in every season of the year. I know how good I feel when it envelops me.

We take a path from Reynaud's house to the shore. I wash my hands in the dark water. I rub my face, run my hands through my hair, and turn to Reynaud, who's standing beside me.

"Thank you . . . for all you've done."

"Of course, Sarah. The hard part comes next."

Then, with a touch of shyness, he asks, "Do you feel up to driving home? You can sleep here if you like."

"I'll be fine. I have to get home to the kids."

"Get some rest. We have a lot to do tomorrow."

Reynaud hands me the bundle of the things we collected today, then gives me a hug. I take a deep breath, holding back my emotions, then I climb into my pickup. I sit there for a moment in a daze without starting the engine, going over the events of the day in my head.

I take a last look at Reynaud, who's already in his house. Through the big windows, I see him take down one of his shotguns. He opens the breech, polishes it, examines the long barrel, and uses a thin brush at the end of a soft rod to clean the barrel.

He, too, is getting ready.

PART THREE:

THE DAUGHTER OF THE LAKE

17

"Long day? You have leaves and twigs in your hair."

As soon as I get home, I collapse on the couch. Karen heard the pickup and immediately made coffee with the cardamon she brought back from her trip to Turkey, which I'd put in the back of a cupboard without ever tasting it. I brush myself off, and she looks at me with a sad expression. I can't even imagine what I look like. Dirty, ugly, wrecked?

"The children didn't squabble too much," Karen continues. "But Hermione is hypersensitive right now. And Benjamin's stammer has gotten worse since the accident, hasn't it?"

I look around at the mess, only half listening to her. I translate "They didn't squabble too much" as "The kids were unbearable."

My house is becoming a real pigsty. I'm going to need more than coffee.

"I patched up the window next to the bookcase. One of the panes was broken. I found some duct tape and a piece of cardboard in the hangar. It'll do for now."

"Thanks, Karen."

"Also, I found a bottle of Dalmore in the garden . . . There's a little left. Would you like some?"

She gives me what she thinks is a conspiratorial smile and puts her hand on mine.

I clench my fist. "The state I'm in, we might as well finish it."

Karen brings two glasses and fills them with what's left in the bottle.

"It's going to take time," she says after a sip, "but I'm sure in time you'll start to feel better . . . even with him gone."

I doubt it. But I want to cut the conversation short. Even she can't bring herself to utter Marceau's name here, in his house. It's still too hard. I raise my glass without further ado and knock the whisky back.

Karen still has that impeccable smile on her face.

I hold the glass to my nose and smell it properly: banana mixed with almond paste. This damn expensive whisky makes me think of a candy apple at a country fair. I put my glass down.

"I'm sorry to ask so much of you right now," I say.

"I know what you're going through. Rollin told me about the safety-deposit box, the money, the manuscript."

I don't say anything about what Reynaud and I discovered. I don't have the strength to go into details.

"Sarah, let me give you a hand with the children."

I look at her with astonishment, slightly offended.

"I know I probably shouldn't interfere . . . but I was tidying things up just to be helpful and . . . I found this."

She's holding Benjamin's report card out to me, open to a specific page. There are several notes intended for me, notes I never read and never signed. Benjamin's temper tantrums in class, two unjustified absences, meals not taken in the cafeteria. I suddenly remember the requests for an appointment his teacher left on my voicemail that I never answered. It was Marceau who always dealt with school matters. I'll have to handle it now, and changing my habits has always been hard.

"Where did you find it?"

"Under the bookcase, when I swept away the pieces of glass."

I've been exposed as a bad mother. It's hard not to feel awful. I've been blind to what's happening in my own house. It's no surprise I never found the report card since I've deleted the word *housework* from my vocabulary. Karen bites her lower lip. Her eyes are still on me. I know what I inspire in her: pity. I've always proudly flaunted my fierce thirst for independence. It was the fighter in me that Marceau loved. What would he think if he saw me today? Would he also feel pity?

"I helped Hermione with her homework," Karen continues. "I know you're both going through a difficult time."

"I can't get through to her these days. If you can, you're lucky. I can pay you to come."

Karen shakes her head. She's stung by my tone.

"After dinner tonight, Hermione suggested we make tea. While she was busy in the kitchen, I went to her room to put away some clothes I'd folded. I noticed a box made by Zoé, you know, the one that Hermione decorated with photos of the three of them camping in the garden last summer."

I'm not in the mood to discuss scrapbooking.

"What did you find, Karen?"

She takes a deep breath.

"Hermione is keeping roll-ups in it. Which don't smell only of tobacco . . ."

I look down at the table.

"We've all done that, Sarah," Karen says. "She'll get over it."

"We didn't do it when we were twelve," I say.

Deep down, what hurts the most is that I'm learning about my daughter's first problems from a friend. Hermione is entering adolescence at a chaotic, stressful moment, and I haven't been there to protect her, to help her.

A few minutes pass. We've run out of things to say.

Karen stands up to leave.

"I have to get up early tomorrow. Try to get some rest. I know you hate not working, but you need to look after yourself. A good warm shower will do you good. Then go straight to bed."

She kisses me and goes, closing the door behind her.

Now I'm even being reminded to take a shower, like a child. Without warning, tears start to flow again. I didn't know I had any left. I feel disgusted with myself. Nausea rises inside me; my face feels flushed with heat. Before I can get to the sink, I throw up on the parquet floor. This is all I needed: more mess to clean up. I hear quiet steps on the stairs going up to the bedrooms. I feel too empty to follow them. This terrible mother will stay huddled in the shadows, then wash everything up, starting with the vomit on her clothes.

~

I start a bath, and before getting in, I decide to look in Marceau's study, searching the shelves and cabinets. Nothing. Not the slightest trace of a manuscript. There's only Marceau's computer, and I haven't been able to get into it. I don't know his password. I try a series of combinations, but nothing works. The woman who knows her man so well she can read his mind and crack his password? I guess that only happens in the movies.

A persistent splashing disturbs my search. The bathroom.

"Shit!"

I run down the corridor. The bath is overflowing. The emergency drain is blocked. Now I know what happened to the bars of soap that kept disappearing. Benjamin must have been using them as modeling clay . . . I clear the plugged drain long enough for the water level to go down; then I slide gently into the tub. My body disappears under the water, but my questions don't go away. Where the fuck is that manuscript?

The warmth of the bath envelops me, and I hold my breath for as long as I can, then come up for air.

I stay in the bathtub while the water empties, the skin on my fingers wrinkled. I allow memories to drift through my mind, memories of days with Marceau, hoping I'll recall something I haven't thought of before. I remember his smell, his smile, his voice, his mouth, our lovemaking . . . It's all too painful.

The soap suds slide down my legs, revealing the tattoo on my right ankle, my one tattoo. It depicts the lake surrounded by mountains with a little plane, the plane Jade begged me not to forget. She'd shown me her drawing the summer before she disappeared, the day Marceau got his pilot's license. Looking at me more intensely than she ever had before, Jade asked me if I wanted to have the drawing tattooed on my right ankle. She would have it done too. I still remember the words that followed:

"Daughters of Lake Geneva, its mountains, and its sky, now that we've had our baptism of air together. Inheritors of my father's dream, a dream revived by Marceau's flight above these waters."

Her voice still echoes in my mind. Getting the matching tattoos meant so much to her. To me too. The lake, the mountains, Jade, and Marceau. We had them done together by the same handsome young guy, who was covered in tattoos from head to foot. I remember he had a crush on Jade, like all the boys.

I have goose bumps and wrap myself in a towel. It's almost midnight. I pull the quilt over me. I slide my hand over the right side of the bed and feel the slight depression in the mattress where Marceau used to sleep by my side. I don't want anyone else to be there. I clench my teeth, waiting for sleep. I feel spasms in my legs, and I'm afraid of what's going to happen next. It's the same every night. I drift into sleep for a few hours; then the nightmare starts: Marceau's hands as he climbs, missing his hold. I see him falling in the empty air, and he reaches out to me, but it's like I've lost control of my body, and I can't catch hold of him. I scream at the top of my lungs. He mouths an answer, but I don't hear what he says. I'm assaulted by images of the summit from our climb today, and the degree of detail in the dream is new and terrifying. Marceau falls away from me. I lean over the cliff edge, and he's struggling in the void, screaming frantically, but it's as if we're separated by a thick, indestructible pane of glass. I can't do anything for him. I can see him, but I cannot hear him. He tries to call out to me again, and I go closer to the edge, desperate to hear him, and with nothing to hold on to, I topple over the edge too. I see Marceau crash onto the ground and disappear. I join him at hair-raising speed. My heart bursts in my chest, I cover my face with my hands, and I find myself sitting bolt upright in bed, bathed in sweat, panting . . .

I get out of bed, as I do almost every night, and walk downstairs and out of the house. Usually, the nightmare fades after a few minutes, but not tonight. I cross the garden, barefoot, then run to the dock, heading straight for the lake, and jump in. The cold water devours me. I let myself sink, my mind still half-asleep, even the shock of the water not enough to bring me back to reality. Engulfed in these dark depths, I can't make out a single thing, not even the bubbles of air as I scream with rage and let myself sink even deeper. The pressure in my ears becomes unbearable. *I'm going to drown.* My lungs are about to open, demanding the air of life. I manage to hold my breath a little longer, bubbles escaping from my mouth.

I am a daughter of the lake, the mountains, and the sky. The lake has always been there for me.

18

THE MANUSCRIPT

Our first summer as guides, Reynaud gave us a few days of obligatory training. He required us to write this down in our notebooks:

"To become a guide, you have to listen, learn, and understand the mountains.

"You will be guiding groups, and you will be responsible for them. Never forget the basic rules, even on routes you use every day. It's always those routes we think we know the best where accidents happen . . ."

We weren't sure Reynaud was talking only about the hiking trails. Passionate as we were, Sarah, Jade, and I didn't take his words that seriously. We were just waiting for the moment when we could abandon our notebooks and lessons, all the dos and don'ts, and finally take advantage of the joys of the lake and the mountains. A lifetime isn't long enough to explore and understand the inexhaustible Lake Geneva area. We would drag our kayaks from shore to shore, over pebbles, over sand, and over lawns depending on the place. We would paddle away from the shore, splashing each other with our paddles. In that game, I often took the lead, except when Sarah and Jade ganged up on me. The daughters of the lake, the daughters of the mountains, and soon, with my pilot's license, the daughters of the sky. I kept my promise and got my pilot's license. And I flew them over the lake.

Even when I was a child, my one dream was to fly. In the kitchen, Dad would entertain Jade and me with stories of flying, until our mother would ask him to come back down to earth. He would pretend to take an interest in dinner, but as soon as the meal was over, he would run to the hangar to clean his Savage Bobber. With its two big front tires, it wasn't its performance he loved, but the way it could take off and land at a very low speed enchanted my father. He took Jade and me flying many times over the lake and the heights of Mont Blanc, which were imprinted in our minds like the maps we studied. On rare occasions, when there were only the two of us on board, my father let me take over the controls. A shiver would run through me, making its way from my fingertips to the back of my neck and deep into my brain: I was really flying! Mother never knew about it, of course. But that evening I told Jade. At the time, I think she felt jealous, but my sister and I shared everything: our secrets, our fears, our greatest joys. No petty envy could have broken our bond.

When my father's Savage Bobber crashed into the lake, the fever he had instilled in me didn't go away. Rather, learning to fly became an obsession. My mother wouldn't let me start taking lessons with an instructor when I turned fifteen, the legal age. I had to wait another year, and I took the exam to get my private pilot's license when I was seventeen. When I came home having passed the test, wearing my flight cap and sunglasses, I could see in her eyes, despite her reticence, that she was proud of me. It was the same pride she used to show my father. In her eyes, I had become an adult, and we were trying to turn the page after my father's death. Despite all my efforts, though, I could never convince her to set foot again in a plane. She would watch us fly over the lake from the house, carrying an anxiety that never left her until the day she died.

When Sarah joined our group of friends, she was an immediate breath of fresh air, like the air winding through the Alpine passes in early spring. Sarah and Jade became unusually close. If it hadn't been for Sarah's Swiss accent, anyone would have taken them for sisters. When I took Jade flying above the lake and the surrounding mountains, I would sometimes close my eyes and let her guide me, just like when we'd run blindfold through the garden as children. We knew each other so well that her eyes, her words, and even the intonations of her voice became mine. She would sometimes place her hands on my shoulders and pilot the plane by proxy. My eyes still closed, I would transpose Jade's pressure on my shoulders into the Savage Bobber's control stick. Before long, Sarah asked if she could come with us, and Jade was genuinely pleased. Sarah was concerned that my passion for flying might create a distance between us. Flying with me, Sarah discovered for the first time the beauty of the place where she'd grown up seen from above. She fell even more in love with it, and I think that love reflected on me too at the time, since I was the one who brought her these experiences. She told me about new places to fly over, telling me all about their histories. She was an open book, and I grew attached to each of her chapters.

A few weeks after our first flight, I noticed the tattoo on Sarah's ankle. The tattoo had yet to heal, and it made sense now why they'd avoided swimming in the lake, even though it was the height of summer. As I looked more closely, I realized with a pang Sarah's tattoo was exactly the same as Jade's.

And Sarah told me . . . her version.

"It's a drawing of us, Jade and me, the daughters of Lake Geneva, water and sky."

It was a double shock. Of course, I didn't let on to Sarah what the tattoo really meant, but later I made Jade promise never to say anything more about that tattoo. She'd put part of our secret on their ankles. It was a risky thing to do.

The bond between Jade and Sarah was so strong, I couldn't object to anything.

In the clear waters, they glided with the ease of silvery fera, those fish emblematic of the lake, undulating gracefully between the invisible currents. On several occasions, Sarah swam across the lake with us. She hadn't always been a swimmer. When she was five, she escaped her parents' supervision, and, convinced she could swim as well as anybody, she jumped off a dock and she sunk like a smooth stone into the water, in almost perfect silence. She claimed she felt completely calm as it happened, even as she dropped a dozen feet down.

The lake couldn't take her, not her.

When she regained consciousness, she was lying on the shore, some twenty yards from the dock. Everyone heaved a great sigh of relief when she came to. Sarah just had a headache and a pain in her scalp. A dog had saved her life, dragging her to shore by her braid. Distraught, Sarah's father had given her chest compressions. She coughed and expelled the water in her lungs and finally concluded that, yes, she knew how to swim.

19

I think I can see dots of light deep inside the icy shadows of the lake. And yet I know it's my uncontrolled movements and the lack of air that are causing these visions. Suddenly, I feel the cold, slippery contact of pebbles covered in plankton and thin seaweed beneath my bare feet. It jolts me, and my reflexes kick in, and I start moving my legs, as much as my weakened muscles allow. I begin my ascent back to the surface, some fifteen feet straight up. The light of the stars and the moon are only visible on the surface. My movements are of a trained swimmer, powerful and precise, but I can feel my muscles weakening, and I have only a few more seconds left of breath before I will not be able to make it to the surface. The pressure on my eardrums is still overpowering, and my movements become jerky. My arms tense up. The darkness around me is still total. I arch my back, my rib cage rising. My head breaks the surface, and in an uncontrollable spasm, I breathe in air and the water running over my face. I feel electricity running through my body. I struggle, splashing, and cough until I'm breathless. The pain is mixed with the fear.

When I get back to the dock, I grip one of the support pilings, my hands sliding over the viscous film of green seaweed. I finally manage to hug the piling, as if clutching a rope to climb. I gradually feel better; my body is coming back to life. Unable to hoist myself onto the dock, I move from piling to piling until I reach the shore and kneel in the grass, shivering. I see a dim light coming from the window of Benjamin's room. It must be his bedside lamp, although I'm pretty sure his light was off when I went to bed.

My legs trembling, I walk through the garden, keeping close to the woods. Dripping with water, I pass my hands through my hair, pushing it out of my face. All of a sudden, I freeze. There is a loud, strange noise a few yards away from me, coming from the dark woods. I consider running, but instead I go a few steps closer. My heart is beating fast. I feel like I'm being watched through the leaves. If it was an animal, it would have run away. And, besides, I'm not afraid of animals. Someone is there, has been there from the start. There's nothing normal about anything that's happening to me. I can't do anything in the darkness, but whatever this is, the danger is quite real. This is not just something I'm imagining. I wait a few seconds longer without moving. After a few moments of silence, the cold and my fatigue get the better of me, and I resume walking back to the house. In less than three hours, the first rays of the sun will rise above the lake.

I drop my wet clothes in the basket next to the washing machine and grab a towel from the heap of laundry that's been waiting for ages to be ironed. The heap collapses. Once I'm dry, I randomly grab some warm clothes. Exhausted as I am, it's impossible to go back to bed. There's no way I'll be able to fall asleep again, with all the adrenaline running through me. I go back to Marceau's study. I am determined to find something there to provide answers to all my questions.

20

KAREN

The clock radio tells me it's four a.m. I've had a restless night, but that was predictable. I stretch a leg to touch Rollin's but don't find it. I turn around. In the darkness and my half-awake state, I can't make anything out, and I don't hear his breathing either. I reach out my arm—the sheet isn't even warm. Completely awake now, I get out of bed. My satin nightdress slides over my skin. There are no lights on in the house, and not the slightest sound. Where the hell is he? I switch the light on in the hall. His coat is there, his shoes too. Then I switch on the light in the living room, and my heart skips a beat.

"What the hell are you doing, sitting in the dark? You scared the life out of me!"

He's on the couch. He doesn't move.

"What's the matter, Rollin?"

"As you can see, I can't sleep."

"Is it because of Marceau's letter?"

"What do you think?"

I have to find out what's behind all this. And keep control. "But you were asleep when I got back from Sarah's."

"I was beat, and I took something. It knocked me out, but it wasn't enough. This manuscript business . . . it's driving me crazy. Marceau and I used to tell each other everything, so why . . . Sarah went berserk. And knowing her, it's not going to end there."

Everyone has secrets. I don't want to find myself discovering things like Sarah, from a third party—too late. So I try to approach the subject carefully.

"There's nothing to fear, Rollin. Or are there things about us in that manuscript?"

My main concern is to protect my family. And I don't know how much I can count on Rollin.

"What can there possibly be, Karen? Just terrible memories, and we don't need those. I don't want . . . the memories to be rehashed, don't you see?"

He's giving me the runaround, but I keep my voice soft. "What does that mean? That we shouldn't look for the manuscript? Tell me, Rollin."

"Sarah wouldn't hear of it; she'd go crazy. But yes, I think it might be best."

"Those things . . . that summer . . . it was before we met. But if there are things you have to tell me, you can. Now. I'd rather hear it from you . . . and if we can avoid problems, that's fine by me. Think of Zoé."

Rollin at last looks up at me, but he doesn't say anything. There's a long silence.

"There's nothing to tell!" he says at last. "It's just . . . that there must be something about Jade. And the way he has of telling a story, a manuscript like that could kill us. That summer, Karen, planted . . . a kind of seed in me, a seed of pain. I was twenty years old, I was terrified, don't you see? It's the kind of thing that happens on TV, or to other people! Not a day passed without the two of us writing to each other. We were an item at the time. I had plans, I . . . and then Jade disappeared and never came back."

"I know, you've told me all this before."

"Karen, without you, I'd still be stuck in a cave. That's why I don't want to find that manuscript. All this is going to make me crazy. Why did Marceau feel the need to drag it all up again?"

"Because he was a writer, and writing was his outlet. Because, like you, there was something he still hadn't processed. Something he never talked about."

I recognize Marceau's angst very well. It was a taboo subject with Sarah, maybe the one thing we never discussed. Jade was Marceau's ghost, but Sarah gave me the impression she couldn't talk about Jade either, as if it might bring back her ghost. But I've seen the photo of Sarah and Jade that she keeps in her handbag. And then there were those times when Marceau and I went out on the lake and he dove deep down into the water. He hadn't accepted his father's death, so Jade's disappearance made things even worse. Marceau was broken inside, and it drove me crazy for him, and also for Sarah, although I never said anything.

Rollin opens his mouth with difficulty, like a fish out of water, and asks feebly, "How was Sarah when you saw her last night?"

"Before or after I told her about Benjamin and Hermione?"

Rollin frowns. "Why do you say that?"

"They're doing a whole lot of stupid things behind her back. And unfortunately, it's been going on for a while. Yesterday, Sarah was devastated. But I couldn't continue hiding from her the fact that her children aren't doing well. To help her, but also because they're friends with Zoé. I don't want our daughter to be dragged into it."

I tell him the whole story and make him promise to keep his mouth shut. It's nobody's business but Sarah's.

"Zoé can be impressionable, I know," Rollin says, "but she listens to you. More than she listens to me, I know. She knows where the boundaries are."

"That's what we think, but she's still a kid."

"Sarah only has us. Alexis, you, and me . . . It's always complicated with children, anyway."

"Yes, she has us . . ."

But above all, Sarah had Marceau. It was thanks to him that I learned more about her, that I learned to understand her better. He was the glue that kept the two of us together.

I've never seen Rollin so worried. What are you going to do now, Sarah? After Marceau, will I lose you too? What consequences does all this have for us—for *me*?

21

I glance at my reflection in the rearview mirror. The whites of my eyes are tinged with red, a mixture of fatigue, sadness, and anger. It isn't yet eight in the morning, and I'm already at the wheel, determined to go through with this. I try to keep my attention on the road. Braking, keeping my distance, looking in the rearview mirror, declutching before changing gears, and at the same time thinking: *This is all a mess.*

In the parking lot outside the police station in Thonon-les-Bains, one of the reserved spots is available, and I grab the opportunity. An officer who's just finishing his cigarette watches me. As I slam the door, he shakes his head and motions me to climb back in. I throw my keys at him, and he catches them in mid-flight, losing his cigarette butt in the process. Taking advantage of his surprise, I hurry into the building. In passing, I slam my identity card down on the desk, which makes the on-duty officer bending over his cell phone look up. I hear him yelling my name, which he's read presumably on my identity card.

Captain Delmas comes out of his office. The officer gesticulates at him, half exasperated, half relieved.

"Where do you think you're going?" Delmas asks.

"Homicide."

"Didn't I make myself clear, or are you having difficulty understanding, Madame Miller?"

"Madame Miller has evidence today. Wasn't that what you wanted?"

"Who do you think you are?" he asks.

"I think I'm someone who will inform the prosecutor if you don't deal with it. Don't for a minute think I won't report you."

"Don't you know anything about rules and procedures, Madame Miller?"

I hand him the envelope, which he angrily grabs.

"You will like this," I say.

"If there's nothing conclusive in here, I'll have you locked in one of our cells, Madame Miller."

Delmas takes out the photos from the surveillance cameras in the bank. His eyes take in the date, time, and place, as well as the red circle drawn in felt-tip pen around what Marceau is holding in his hand. He looks in the envelope and sees there's more.

"In my office," he says.

I sit down opposite him, ready for the second round. His pencil holder has been patched with Scotch tape. Out of caution, he moves it closer to him.

"If you get the slightest desire to throw anything, it's the cell. OK?"

"That's entirely up to you, Captain Delmas."

"Don't push me, Miller. Don't push me."

He scrutinizes the records of Marceau's visits to the bank. His right eyebrow lifts. He's puzzled by the timing. Nothing for more than a year, and then a visit a few weeks before his death. Delmas takes out the transparent bag containing the climbing sling we found on the Dent du Vélan. An official bag, carefully marked, as you're taught to do in the police academy. I can see he finds that fishy. He looks up at me.

"What is this?"

"I told you, there are some things I'm quite capable of doing."

Suspiciously, he inspects the contents of the bag. With his fingers, he presses the material in a specific place. He frowns, then taps on the large window to the room where his team has their desks. He gestures to one of his officers, who immediately comes to the door of Delmas's office.

"Captain?"

Delmas hands the officer the transparent bag. "This mark here, on the label . . . Do you think it might have anything to do with that robbery a few months ago? Can you check it for me?"

The officer turns the object over and gives a slight smile.

"I can confirm it straightaway. It's the same kind. Where did it come from?"

"Madame Miller just brought it in."

I'm on the edge of my seat. Either Reynaud and I screwed up and this has to do with another case entirely, or we have something.

"What's all this about a robbery?" I ask.

With a glance at his officer, Delmas says, "About six months ago, the plant room of the Forest Center was burglarized. Nothing valuable was taken, and there wasn't much damage. It was kids who did it, twelve-year-olds. They had a key. You can see them in the security footage, but it isn't possible to really identify them. The quality of the footage is poor, and they were wearing masks. They mainly took candy that was being saved for a party they were planning, as well as some of the gear. Quite practical, these kids. But for some years now, the Forest Center has been putting a small mark in indelible ink on the labels of its gear. Like a signature."

The Forest Center. Our youth, Marceau's and mine, suddenly resuscitated. At the same time, I recall what Karen told me last night. What if my own kids took part in this stupid prank? Thinking of Hermione and Benjamin being involved in this would be too much. Suddenly my determination withers.

"As it says on the bag, the sling was found near the place where my husband was killed. There are also traces on the summit of the rock face Marceau was climbing, and beekeepers in the vicinity noticed a vehicle there just before Marceau's death. The area will need to be searched again. And by the way, I didn't find anything in his study—no manuscript, no memory stick, no backup. Except maybe the printer—I read in the instructions that it's possible to check the performance history. But I don't have access to my husband's laptop. I don't have the password."

I've let go of this almost in one breath, as if freeing myself of it. Delmas's face has clouded over. Without taking his eyes off me, he tilts his head back slightly, then to the side.

"It's that old madman Reynaud who's behind all this, isn't it?"

I feel like slapping him and tearing out his beady crow eyes. This time, I'm the one who tilts my head, but forward, straight at him.

"I'll be after you until you launch an investigation."

"It isn't up to you. You can't just come in here and tell me how to do my job."

"Let me help you, damn it!"

"Out! Get out of my office now!"

I glare at him.

"My mind is made up. Marceau had a lot of important contacts, a very full address book. I am finally going to put it to good use."

This is just the beginning for Delmas . . .

22

There is only one person whose love has always been there for me, a genuine love without judgment: my grandmother Louise.

In her presence I can breathe calmly, abandon my questions and doubts for a while, like suitcases at the back of a closet, and get her sincere, generous, undivided attention. I can lower my defenses without fearing any immediate danger.

On the hills above Évian, I drive with the windows down, intoxicated by the scent of the freshly cut hedges, the well-tended lawns, the fragrant mixture of honeysuckle, heliotrope, and four o'clock flowers. Above the roofs, between the houses and the vegetation, the lake and the immensity of the mountains can be seen in the background. I climb the Avenue de la Dent d'Oche, heading for the care home where my grandmother lives. From her room, she can keep an eye on the lake, the mountains, and the forest. It's there, in the Alzheimer's unit, that she fills notebooks all day long with her diary.

I leave the pickup in the visitors' parking lot and climb the familiar stairs. The nurse's aides greet me. At this hour, my grandmother isn't yet out and about in the communal rooms or the garden. I knock at her door, according to our ritual, and look at my children's drawings, which have been Scotch taped under the room number 27. I wait for Louise's voice, the signal to enter.

"Only the door is crazy, not Granny Louise." For a ninety-two-year-old, her voice is steady.

Everyone calls her Granny Louise here. Her smile overwhelms me with its warmth. She's sitting in her armchair near the big window. Her skin tells the story of the most beautiful years of my life—all its lines are memories. The room is simple but pretty. Nobody is surprised that there's a successful writer in her family, given the number of writing notebooks piled up in her closet and on the furniture.

"Did you know they've cut down the trees near the church. What are the birds supposed to do? It was wonderful to see them fly off every time the bell rang." She's indignant but not resigned. "Anyway, I see a little more of the lake like this. But I'll call the town hall to complain, all the same."

I've brought her a pebble I collected from the shore of the lake. It's been our habit for years now. She takes it, runs her finger along a white vein on the dark gray of the pebble, typical of the lake, and sniffs it. The verdict is always the same . . .

"It smells good. Definitely comes from our lake, this one."

She always wants me to tell her exactly where I found a new pebble, what day, at what time. She notes this information down in her exercise book, then adds a number under the pebble. Then she tells me what she knows about the place the pebble comes from, what experiences she's had there.

In her exercise books, apart from her diary, she keeps a meticulous record of every pebble, and then she spends hours in the painting studio decorating the stones. When she's done, she places them in the flower beds in front of the care home.

Sitting in her armchair, Louise holds her arms out to me. I get down on my knees and place my head in her lap. She strokes my hair like she did when I was a child. For a while, I close my eyes and forget the world. I feel her gnarled but still nimble fingers moving through my hair, touching my scalp, which immediately calms me.

"You must tell Marceau to visit. He usually comes every week and tells me how his book is going, but it's been a while since I last saw him."

I feel a pang in my heart. She's forgotten. That's how it is with Louise. She can be happy several times in the same day with the same good news, and she can be sad too, not only about bad news but because she realizes from time to time that her memory is failing her. As the years have passed, even the exercise books, the diaries, and the pebbles are falling by the wayside.

Trying to change the subject, I talk to her about Benjamin and Hermione. I show her new photos on my phone. The kids also visit regularly and bring their own pebbles. I don't mention Marceau.

"You should be at work at this time of day, Sarah! Go, don't leave Karen alone."

She hasn't completely lost her memory.

"I only made a little detour to come see you, Grandmother, but I'll be back soon."

"Don't forget to tell Marceau to come. I want to continue my diary. And try to get some rest. You look tired."

There's a tightness in my throat, but I don't give in to the sadness until I leave the room. My phone is vibrating in my pocket, diverting my attention. It's the person I contacted after searching through the hundreds of business cards I found in Marceau's study. We've agreed to meet on the terrace of a restaurant in the harbor in Yvoire. The woman's voice is confident, professional. She's already waiting for me.

~

In the medieval town of Yvoire, every stone bears witness to its history. I drive through two ancient pillars with a rusted metal gate. The walls of the town, although still sturdy, bear the scars of time, of wars.

The narrow cobblestone streets wind between centuries-old buildings, a labyrinth of shadow and light. The facades of the half-timbered houses, some dating back to the fourteenth century, are adorned with scarlet geraniums, jasmine, and honeysuckle, which fill the air with their scent. The stained-glass windows cast multicolored reflections on the cobbled ground. I try to draw the strength I need from this beauty, the strength I'm lacking.

Across a small square, there's a granite fountain carved with floral motifs. Around it, café tables invite you to stop and taste a local wine while listening to the hubbub of conversations and the laughter of children playing hide-and-seek behind the statues.

Farther on, the Garden of the Five Senses is a haven of peace, bright with colors and fragrances. Roses, their colors ranging from dark red to pale pink, vie with lavender, iris, and day lilies. Butterflies whirl about with delight, letting themselves be carried by the gentle breeze.

I drink all this in, allowing it to intoxicate me.

As I descend toward the harbor, the lake offers an incomparable view of its seductive blue expanse. A deep indigo, glistening in the sun, like sapphires. The majestic swans of Yvoire glide over the water, and in the harbor, elegant sailboats mingle with fishing boats, looking as if they are suspended over the crystal-clear water. The only thing missing from this beautiful scene is Marceau.

Here, past and present merge.

I searched across the square for the journalist I have planned to meet. I spot her. She looks just as she described herself: dark hair, light-colored blouse, sunglasses, sitting at a table in the shade. I walk unsteadily toward her and notice her looking at me up and down. I'm probably not the way she imagined the wife of a successful novelist would look. I feel uneasy in her gaze. Marceau was so much better at dealing with journalists.

I hand her a flash drive, as agreed. We spend more than an hour together, she pays the bill, and then we walk along the harbor for a while longer. Finally, she holds out her hands to thank me.

Now the ball is rolling.

~

On the way to Lugrin, I find myself compulsively checking the rearview mirror. I swear the car following me is the same one that was parked not far from me in Yvoire. The man at the wheel is wearing sunglasses, and he's totally nondescript. About a hundred yards ahead, I spot a wide space on the edge of a cornfield, an access way for agricultural machinery. Without signaling, I abruptly turn off the road onto the farm track, raising a cloud of dust. As the air clears, I hear the engine of the man's car come closer, then slow down as he passes, staring at me, then waves. I may sound crazy, but I keep my hands tight on the wheel. I try to breathe in calmly, but my nerves are in shreds. I feel like I'm living through one endless day—one long nightmare with false moments of rest, overwhelmed by the terrible feeling that everything and everyone is against me.

Leaving the engine on, I get out of the truck and walk around it, getting some air, kicking each tire as I pass it. I wish I could scream, let go of my rage, my frustrations, my grief, but nothing comes. It's impossible to purge these unbearable feelings. I get back in the truck and drive past the last houses in Lugrin and plunge back into the forest. My eyes catch a sudden reflection in the narrow entrance of a side road I've just passed. The hood of a car? I'm almost sure it is. But everything's going too fast, and I continue on, keeping my eyes on the rearview mirror until the turnoff that leads to Reynaud's house. Strangely, I feel safer in the forest. As I pull up near the house, I'm filled with a mixture of doubt, anxiety, and false logic. I'm worried maybe I am going crazy. Reynaud is on his terrace. He smiles at me and turns the screen of his laptop toward me. It was a retirement gift, and by now he knows how to use it.

"Already!" I say.

"It's all over the media. Look: 'Crime or accident? What really happened to bestselling writer Marceau Miller?' And this: 'It's looking increasingly unlikely that writer and mountaineer Marceau Miller met his death as the result of an accident.'"

Reynaud is smiling broadly now. I told the journalist in Yvoire everything—a good alternative to upsetting the knickknacks on Delmas's desk. As Reynaud continues to list the media outlets that have taken up the story, confirming that it's become a national affair, I notice a large easel set up on the terrace.

"Are you taking up painting now as well as hunting?"

Reynaud closes his laptop, gets to his feet, and disappears inside the house. I follow him, glancing at the photographs on the cabinet under the window. The one of Jade is no longer there. Reynaud returns and motions me to move aside. He's carrying a board nearly five feet long. He places it on the easel. I can't believe my eyes.

"We're going to go right back to the beginning, Sarah. I used this board for years when I was working on cases."

"So, as far as you're concerned, retirement is just a concept?"

He waves a hand in the air dismissively. Obviously, I'm delighted. Among the photographs and documents already pinned to the board is the photo of Jade. There's also one of me, dating from the spring, on board a boat on the lake. There are photos of Karen, Rollin, Alexis, and the children too. Reynaud begins commenting on each of them, one by one, but the noise of a car engine interrupts him.

"Are you expecting someone?" Reynaud asks.

I shake my head.

"Nobody ever comes here at this hour."

Reynaud goes back inside to get a shotgun from the three hanging on the wall. I stay on the terrace ready to greet whoever it is.

23

A police car with its lights flashing pulls up behind my pickup. Delmas slams the car door as he gets out and strides toward me, followed by an officer with broad shoulders.

"Are you completely oblivious? You've just stirred up a hornet's nest!"

"Am I to assume that the investigation is now on, Captain?"

I see Delmas's face turn red; the veins on his neck and forehead swell. The black in his eyes is like the ink of a cuttlefish.

"I have the prosecutor at my throat. The station has turned into a call center. People are coming from all over the country! The station parking lot is overrun with reporters; they're knocking on the doors and windows. All the hotels are filling up—some people are even camping out! You're going to screw everything up! It's all anyone is talking about, and it's my team that's bearing the brunt."

The officer accompanying Delmas leans toward him and shows him his cell phone.

"Wonderful!" Delmas cries. "That's all we need. Your husband's fans have created a support page on social media, 'The Truth About the

Death of Marceau Miller.' His publisher has already shared it, and so has at least one newspaper!"

He turns to me. "Next I expect to see hordes of women readers trampling all over the evidence."

He's not only arrogant, he's a misogynist. All the things I like. The other officer approaches him again.

"Chief, the mayor is asking to see you urgently. He wants to hold a press conference to reassure the public."

Delmas is only half listening. He's staring at Reynaud. The captain's phone is sure to run out of battery soon—it's vibrating constantly with a flood of messages and calls. Delmas and Reynaud look each other up and down. The captain ends up looking down at the shotgun; then his eyes grow wide when he spots the display board.

"What are you doing? Tell me I'm dreaming!"

"It's always bothered you having me around, hasn't it, Delmas? I guess when you don't do your job properly, you end up getting caught out."

"I respect you as a veteran, but you were in the job too long. A person should know when to give up. And right now, you don't have any authority in this case, do you understand? I'm not going to tell you a second time!"

Reynaud takes his time before replying. "Delmas, if you fuck up this case, your career will never recover. Take my word as a veteran. You're in the media spotlight. You'll be the first to go if you don't get a grip on the investigation. It's your head that's on the line, not mine."

Delmas's masked resentment cracks. The observation hits home, and Reynaud has him by the balls. A slight smile hovers over the older man's lips, a smile of unfeigned satisfaction. He's the master of the game now.

"Don't do anything else without informing me," Delmas says, trying to save face. "The investigation is open. From now on, whatever you do counts as an obstruction of justice. I don't want to come here again."

Delmas and his associate get back in their car and reverse noisily.

I look at Reynaud. I have the feeling I'm reliving the past, twenty years later, a new tragedy, and with the same sense that we won't get to the bottom of what happened. A chilly silence descends on us. Reynaud takes the cartridge from the shotgun and places the weapon on the terrace table. He rolls the cartridge in the palm of his hand and stares at it. This is the moment I choose to tell him about my intuition. And my intentions.

"You know . . . what happened that summer, with Jade . . . To be honest, I never believed it. Of course, I trusted Marceau completely. But I need to understand, I must. Deep down I'm convinced that Marceau's death is linked to his sister's disappearance . . ."

Reynaud is silent for a moment before replying. "It isn't as simple as that, Sarah. Jade's case is closed, and we need new evidence directly linked to it to reopen the investigation. We can't just go on intuition."

I move close to him.

"Don't give me that police bullshit. You have to get a handle on this. For me, for Marceau, for Jade, and for yourself. Fuck Delmas. I don't give a fuck about his threats."

Reynaud lowers his head. He seems to be struggling. He finally says, in a thin voice that doesn't sound like him, "I don't know where I screwed up, Sarah. I looked at everything. I explored every lead for years. There was nothing, nothing at all. It was as if she'd vanished into thin air. It's been eating away at me for twenty years."

Then Reynaud suddenly gets to his feet and asks me to follow him. In the back of the house, behind a heap of firewood nine feet high, he gets down on his knees. I now see there's a trapdoor with a big padlock on it like the entrance to a bomb shelter. Reynaud opens the door wide and flips a switch. He motions me to go in before him. I go down, taking care on the steep steps.

The cellar extends under the entire house. On one side, there are stone alcoves filled with bottles of wine, and further on, a workbench covered with tools. Beyond a narrow corridor, lit by a weak light bulb, there is a door covered by what looks like armor plating with a heavy lock and a yellow-and-black logo: the nuclear symbol.

Reynaud unlocks this metal door, and we enter a dark room with no echo. Sounds are completely muffled, like the silence of long-held secrets. Even a scream would not be heard from outside.

24

THE MANUSCRIPT

We all have a secret garden, some bigger than others.

But who knows how long a secret lasts? Sarah knows the entrance to my garden. I've thrown away the key, but the gate is open.

It wasn't long before I needed space, needed to go breathe other air. The first time it happened, not knowing how to broach the subject and, above all, not wanting to meet with a refusal, I ran away. It was a few months after my father died. I was about ten. I left a note on my bed: "I'll be back tomorrow." So, the first day, my mother waited. The second day, inevitably, she went to the police. It was Reynaud, not yet a captain at the time, who was entrusted with the task of finding me. Reynaud was a relatively young officer then, not yet forty. He tracked me down in less than twenty-four hours, which I have to say was somewhat maddening. I had made sure to stay away from the well-marked tracks and had buried myself deep in the forest. It was as if Reynaud had a sixth sense. My mother had been right to contact the police.

Rather than lecture me, Reynaud didn't judge me. He was like the forest, ready to welcome me without worrying about who I was, and that was fine with me. I had taken a bag with me, containing what I needed to sleep, eat, drink, and read. A real scout. But I had forgotten how many mosquitoes there are in summer. That was how my forest apprenticeship began.

There, at least, nobody talked about my father's death. I could pretend it never happened, which was a relief. Reynaud taught me the basics, suitable for a boy of ten, except that I caught on quicker than most. Gradually, the forest became my home away from home. Over the years, my mother stopped worrying when I disappeared from time to time. She knew it was something I needed to do. I always left the same note, "I'll be back," and I always was. My mother didn't talk about it to me, or to anybody else, for that matter.

Jade would stay home. She knew why I left, but we didn't need to talk about it. When I started to work as a guide for the Forest Center, I hid from everybody the fact that I already knew the forest better than Reynaud himself. Even Jade didn't suspect how much. In order not to be noticed, I would express the same amazement as everyone else, pretend to fall into the same traps as Jade or Sarah, and write conscientiously in my notebook, just like the others. I was dying to either approve or refute some of what Reynaud said, but I kept it all to myself.

One more secret.

But the forest knew. It was like a silent dialogue between the forest and me, and it never betrayed me. On the contrary, it was my greatest ally.

The forest is alive, like us, but far superior in intelligence. It lives at its own rhythm. It adapts to the environment, whereas we try to adapt the environment. We aren't aware of a fraction of the animals that prowl around us in the woods, unless we've been taught to do so. Our senses have been corroded by civilization. Soon our sense of touch will know nothing but the contact of industrial products. The primitive capacities of our sense of smell are asleep, led astray by chemical odors. Our sense of sight is being reduced and no longer reacts to anything but pixels, a massive injection of artificial light that creates deceptive information for our brain. We have lost our mastery of precious skills, especially skills that help us to defend ourselves and get our bearings.

Sarah has that in her, like a virus we share.

Only, I am more affected than she is. That's the abyss she sometimes glimpses in my eyes, without fully understanding it. I am of this world, but not completely.

25

I keep moving forward in the half light of Reynaud's bunker. He flicks another switch, and light bursts from a line of bulbs hanging from the ceiling. The walls are covered with maps of the region and photographs that are familiar to me, but also drawings, diagrams, and climbing and hiking material.

"Twenty years of investigation, Sarah. For twenty years I've been looking, for twenty years I've been doubting, for twenty years I've been trying to understand, for twenty years I've been trying to keep believing in the impossible."

It takes me several long minutes to understand what I'm seeing. My eyes move from wall to wall, taking in every detail. There's one drawing in particular, a pencil drawing of a face. I run my hand over it. I'm speechless.

"Four years ago, I asked a portrait artist to create what Jade might look like today, based on photographs."

I look closely at this image, then at all of the other photographs. I take down one. I don't ask any questions, and Reynaud knows perfectly well what questions are going through my mind. And among all of them, *the* question.

"I don't know why Marceau didn't want me to tell you," he says at last. "I think it's because of the guns. He didn't want to frighten you. He thought you might stop him."

In the photograph, Marceau is posing with Reynaud, each carrying a shotgun. I look at my husband's face to make sure it really is Marceau.

"We only hunted very occasionally. The purpose *wasn't* hunting, Sarah, it was always to search for the slightest trace of Jade. Where we went, I doubt any hunter had ever set foot before."

"So why take shotguns?"

"We had them for security more than anything else. All I can say is that even though I was one of the best shots in our group, I rarely hit my target. Marceau, on the other hand, never missed. He had a gift for it. He had much quicker reflexes than me. By the time I turned, he was already taking aim."

I probe my memory, mentally processing hundreds of situations at lightning speed. "So, when he went off into the forest, it was with you?"

"I didn't always go with him. He didn't tell me everything, you know. Sometimes he'd borrow one of my guns, and he came back with the same number of cartridges."

I look around. There are cardboard boxes overflowing with case documents and test results.

"Where did you and Marceau go? I mean, what places did you explore?"

Reynaud takes a map out of one of the boxes and unfolds it on a workbench. It's almost completely covered with marks in felt-tip pen. I unfold another and another. The map is covered with marks with dates written in tiny handwriting. I pull out a stool near a doorless wardrobe and sit down. Reynaud puts a hand on my shoulder.

"Are you all right, Sarah? Would you like a drink? I have a few bottles down here."

My gaze comes to rest on a corner of the room, where there's a camp bed with a blanket rolled up in a ball.

"Officially, I was ordered to wrap up the investigation. Unofficially, I was continuing one way or another."

"Why didn't you and Marceau ever tell me?"

Reynaud looks at me like a fragile animal. "Because some people have to turn the page to stop from going crazy."

This phrase and its implications echo in me for a long time. I get up from the stool, still shaken. I run my hands over the shelves, probe the boxes one after the other. Once again, I linger over the photographs of Marceau pinned to the wall. I am more than ever convinced that Marceau died because of what happened to Jade. There's a link.

"Who knew about your searches in the forest? Your 'hunting' expeditions?"

"Nobody. At any rate, we saw almost nobody. Where we went, everything was much too wild and isolated."

I continue my questions. I'm looking for something, but I don't know what.

"Did you ever get the feeling you were being followed?"

Reynaud pauses, sits down, and lets his gaze wander over the walls. "No, not that I recall. When you have radar like Marceau's, nobody could have followed us without his noticing."

Under a pile of old hard drives that look as if they haven't been used for a long time, a metal box draws my attention.

"It'll take you hours to open everything, Sarah."

I open the box, and the contents spill onto the shelf. More photographs. I look at them one by one.

Jade with Reynaud on the shore of the lake, arms around each other's shoulders. Jade on a path, smiling brightly, next to Reynaud. Jade and Reynaud in a canoe. Jade in the forest, looking straight at the camera, the top button of her blouse undone. Jade, Jade again, always Jade, suggestive, naked, coming out of the lake . . . along with Reynaud. About thirty photographs in all.

I look at him, dumbstruck. He, too, has frozen.

"You weren't supposed to see these, Sarah."

I realize suddenly that I'm in a bomb shelter in the cellar of an isolated house, unearthing secrets about people I thought I knew. Alone with a man I thought I knew.

I throw down the photos and start running. I hear my name called three times behind me as I climb the steps, emerge from the hole, and close the trapdoor behind me, trying to slow him down. In the open air, I stumble and collapse on the ground next to the log pile, and I can't get up. I gasp for air, crawling on my hands and knees, trying to breathe.

Jade was like a sister to me. We shared everything. At least I thought so. Everything I thought I could trust is giving way, literally and figuratively, like a line of dominoes. Behind me, I hear Reynaud's fists on the metal of the closed trapdoor.

26

I move forward on all fours, the palms of my hands on fire from the rough earth. I get to my feet and run as best I can to the pickup. I take the keys from my pocket; they fall from my shaking hands; I pick them up. I can't get the key in the lock, scratching the paint before I manage to get inside. I start the engine. It's temperamental, but this time it works. I accelerate hard, sending a spray of dirt from the tires. I keep an eye on the rearview mirror as I set off down the forest path. Gathering speed, I start to think I'm going to make it when I see Reynaud at the side of the road, emerging from the high ferns. I drive even faster, passing him, until Reynaud finally disappears from view.

As I rejoin civilization, my phone emits a series of beeps, signaling the arrival of messages. I'll listen to them later. I only want one thing: to get home.

~

At last, my refuge.

The respite is short-lived. As I approach, I make out an unusual amount of activity in front of the house. A trickle of anxiety runs through my veins. A police car is parked next to Karen's. I park the pickup and walk along the drive to the front door. There, a strange welcoming committee is waiting for me: two police officers. One next to the hangar, inspecting Marceau's plane, and the other on the dock at the bottom of the garden. Karen waves while Benjamin runs toward me. Hermione remains sitting on the couch on the terrace next to Zoé, both absorbed by their phones.

"Wh-why are you d-dirty like that, M-Mom?" Benjamin asks.

I brush off my jeans, but I can't get the mud off. I look at my hands, encrusted with dirt, worse than if I'd been gardening without gloves.

When I look up, Karen's look of compassion horrifies me. It's only now that I notice Captain Delmas near the front door. I stroke Benjamin's hair. I try to reassure him, despite this police presence, despite . . . despite me.

"I did some gardening today without getting changed. Not a good idea."

Benjamin doesn't seem convinced.

Karen turns her back on Delmas and whispers to me, "They went to the agency before coming here. I closed it for the afternoon. I'll take care of the kids, don't worry."

Hermione doesn't even look at me. Karen tugs at Zoé's sleeve, and she deigns to greet me. An officer crouches next to her.

"I like your cap."

Zoé doesn't understand. A shiver runs down my spine as I remember the robbery committed by kids at the Forest Center and what the cops said about the caps they wore.

"Where did you buy it?"

"My father gave it to me. He has a food truck, the best food in the area."

Karen puts her arm around her daughter's shoulders and moves her slightly away from the officer, like a lioness protecting her cub.

"My husband had a whole bunch made to promote his business. Why did you ask?"

"I shared them," Zoé cuts in. "I gave some to Hermione and Benjamin."

The officer looks at me. Now I'm on the defensive.

"May I borrow your daughter's cap?" the officer asks Karen.

Karen throws me a glance. Then everything happens fast: Zoé dashes off, taking us all by surprise.

"Zoé! Zoé!" Karen calls, running after her daughter across the lawn.

She catches up with Zoé, but she wouldn't have gotten much farther anyway—there's another officer standing at the bottom of the garden. Karen tries to stop Zoé, but she struggles.

"I didn't do anything! I didn't do anything! I didn't do anything!"

Now she's crying hysterically. The officer picks up the cap, which has flown off during Zoé's mad run. Karen comes to me, Zoé clinging to her.

"Can you explain what's going on, Sarah?"

I no longer know who should lash out at whom at this rate, so I share what I know.

"A while ago, the Forest Center was broken into. The surveillance footage shows a bunch of kids, all wearing the same hats, apparently. You can't see their faces."

Zoé has stopped pushing away her mother's arms.

"So there's no knowing who took part or whose idea it was," Karen says, then abruptly leaves, taking Zoé and my children. From her tone, I guess she's upset, and we'll have to have an unpleasant conversation sooner or later. But right now, so many things are in a jumble inside me, I can't deal with it.

Delmas examines the cap, throwing me regular glances. He's waiting to speak to me, that's clear.

"How did you get all that mud on you? Have you been digging up corpses?"

Adrenaline, fear, and exhaustion are seething in my veins. But I somehow still find the strength to respond. "At a hunting and fishing workshop with your old colleague."

"I told you to stop aiding and abetting him. Do you understand? Do you know where it can lead?"

I open the door to the house. I'm dreaming of my room, of changing my clothes, of being at home. I hand the keys to Delmas.

"The long key is for the cellar, the one with the piece of cloth is for the utility room. Marceau's study is on the second floor."

Delmas gathers his men, who take care to wipe their feet on the doormat before coming in and glance at me as if apologizing for their big dirty boots. But I don't care. I hurry to the kitchen and scrub my nails with a brush at the sink for several minutes. The sound of the water drowns out the sobs that have finally caught up with me.

I rinse my face, rub away my tears, then grab the cloth and dry my cheeks and my hands. I go upstairs to my bedroom, intending to change my filthy jeans. Looking in the mirror, I see a much older version of myself.

In the upstairs hall, the police are going through everything. One of them passes with a pile of cardboard boxes from Marceau's study. I shut myself in Benjamin's room. At least there I won't see their comings and goings. I sit down on the bed. How long has it been since I took a good look at his room? I clean up without lingering, changing the sheets, vacuuming, putting away his clean clothes. Now it's been a while since I've even emptied his waste-paper basket. The animated film posters have been replaced by the heroes of video games and famous athletes. On top of the dresser, the peak of a cap sticks out. Standing on tiptoe, I reach for it with my fingertips. Then a long arm comes past me and grabs the cap. I turn to a police officer who has come up behind me.

"It's definitely the same as his friends'. So, you see, he didn't lose it . . ."

The sight of a uniformed officer in my son's bedroom, holding what I'm sure he thinks is a piece of incriminating evidence, terrifies me.

"Captain Delmas is asking for you, Madame Miller. He's in your husband's study."

I breathe wearily. Before leaving the room, I stop in the doorway and say, my tone one of command rather than entreaty, "I want to speak to my children before you question them. Don't do anything without my permission."

The officer nods as he stuffs the cap into a transparent bag. I walk along the hall to Marceau's study, feeling that I'm being crushed by everything that's happening.

Delmas is wearing white latex gloves. One of his men is taking photographs uninterruptedly. Another is sitting in front of Marceau's computer.

"You say you don't have the password, Madame Miller?"

"That's right."

"We've taken only what we think will be useful," Delmas says.

I look at Marceau's study in a different light now, as if it reflects a truth I don't know, any more than I know Marceau's other secrets. Everything suddenly seems alien to me.

"In your husband's computer, we found files relating to the purchase of an external backup system called Time Capsule. Obviously, a writer must have a backup of some kind."

"As I told you, I didn't find anything. No external hard drive, no memory stick, and certainly not your Time-whatever-it-is system."

"There was a device standing right here, Madame Miller; you can see the circle of dust around it. You can even see where the wire was. Don't you remember anything about it?"

I shake my head. But right now, I'm doubting everything, even myself. The officer who's supposed to be the expert is bent over the printer, manipulating the settings, connecting it to a computer he's brought.

"I've recovered the list of files printed in the last six months, Captain."

Delmas leans over the screen and motions for me to come closer. He scrolls through the file names. They're in every format: JPEG, DOCX, PDF. Some of the files have been given evocative titles, "Psychology," "Medical" . . . And then, dated the day after he went to HSBC: *The Story of Marceau Miller*, a file in docx format, followed by a mixture of about ten numbers and letters, like a serial number. Typical computer gobbledygook.

"*The Story of Marceau Miller*," Delmas says. "That's strange, isn't it? Is that what he called all his books in progress?"

"I have no idea. Only his publisher could confirm that."

"And all these numbers and letters? A date, a reference to something?"

"I really don't know. He never told me anything about his work in progress."

"I see . . . Do you have the telephone number of his publisher, Madame Miller?"

Of course I have it. Whenever he couldn't reach Marceau, Édouard Payet went through me. Delmas takes the number and calls.

"I'm putting it on speaker. I'll almost certainly need you too."

At the second ring, Édouard picks up.

"Captain Delmas of the Thonon-les-Bains police."

"Hello. I was expecting your call."

"I'm calling you to—"

"Yes, I'm following the investigation. You know, it's all over the media. It's terrible, what happened. What about Sarah, how's she bearing up?"

I haven't heard Édouard's voice since he expressed his condolences and sent me a document to sign allowing for the publication of the novel in progress.

"Madame Miller is following our conversation," Delmas replies. "I have a few questions to ask you. Was Marceau Miller working on anything lately? Did he tell you anything about a title, or the subject of his next book, or what he was researching?"

"Marceau was very discreet. He kept a lot of things to himself. I let him get on with it because he always handed in the work on time, which is rare in this business. Marceau was a workaholic; he always had something he was writing. He sent me the first version of the book just over three months ago. That was the way we always did it. It was only then that I read the new novel—when he had a complete text to submit to me, never before."

I realize that even Édouard didn't know much about the genesis of Marceau's work. My husband was even more solitary than I had known.

Frowning, Delmas continues with his questions. “What if I say to you, *The Story of Marceau Miller*? Is that a working title he gave his manuscripts, during that first stage?”

“What a weird idea! Marceau wasn’t quite that self-obsessed. Have you ever read any of his novels? I can send you some. No, he never gave them a title. That was always my job. A title is very important; it’s part of the marketing strategy.”

“What was he working on?”

“That’s confidential, Captain. You must realize, I’ve not only lost a friend, I’ve lost my most important client. Do you know how many copies we sold of his previous book? Come on, say a figure.”

“All I need to know is the subject of his last book, Monsieur Payet.”

“Three hundred and twenty-five thousand copies! In trade format! Do you know how huge that is?”

He never changes. Figures, strategy . . . Even when he’s in mourning, Édouard is still a publisher.

“Édouard,” I cut in, “this is Sarah. It’s very important for the investigation that we know what Marceau was working on.”

“Well, I don’t want to see the subject come out in the press! The manuscript is under contract. I’m paying a ghostwriter a fortune to finish the job; we talked about it, Sarah. All right . . . I’ll tell you . . .”

In my head I’m already somewhere else. At the foot of the mountain of secrets that my husband has left behind.

27

The police have gone, taking away a few more boxes and Marceau's computer. I'm still sitting on Marceau's chair, letting the noises of the garden and the nearby woods drift into the house. Around me, a total mess. Everything has been searched, clothes and objects spilled out of shelves and closets. Like a sheet that's been pulled off a bed, every secret exposed. Except that I can't see it, even though I'm Marceau's wife.

A text from Karen.

Do you want me to keep the kids tonight?

I hesitate for a moment.

I'll pick them up in an hour, thanks, Karen.
I need to talk to them.

What words can a mother find to say in such circumstances? Should I come down on them for the stupid things they've done? Tell them that their acts may have a connection with what happened to their father?

"It's all going to be fine, children. We'll find out who killed Dad . . . and why."

I ought to be terrified at finding myself alone in the house, with the possibility of Reynaud prowling around, but strangely enough, I don't feel anything. I didn't tell Delmas about Reynaud. He would really think I'm a madwoman, and I can't afford that when he's finally launched an investigation.

I close my eyes. Five minutes. I just need five minutes.

~

In Marceau's study, it's starting to get dark. I notice glimmers of light on the ceiling. It's weird—I've almost never been in here. I recognize the phosphorescent stars that Benjamin liked so much. Did he ask his father to cover the ceiling of his study with them? Then, for some reason, my eyes are drawn to the ventilation grille. I move my chair just under the grille and climb up. There's no dust on it, and I notice that one of the four screws holding it in place is missing and the other three are loose enough for me to unscrew them by hand. I drop the screws on the floor, one by one, and pull out the grille. Thankfully, I am not afraid of spiders, like Hermione, or I'd have to put on gloves and grit my teeth to put my hands into the space above the ceiling. I grope, unable to see what I'm doing, until my fingers come up against a heavy object. Holding my breath, I grab one end and pull it out.

It's a handgun, the metal cold to the touch. I get off the chair, upset that Marceau had a gun like that under our roof, where our children could have found it. He understood how careless children can be . . .

Then it occurs to me that, given everything that's happening, maybe I should at least learn how it works.

Still holding the gun, I continue inspecting the room, as if the gun is the first clue in a treasure hunt and there are other discoveries to be made. Suddenly I hear someone knocking at the front door. I look out through the window of the study. It's almost dark outside, but the sensor light has been activated, and I make out a figure. It isn't Karen. Then I see the hood of a red Porsche parked on the lawn. Cursing, I go downstairs and open the door.

"Hello, Sarah. You didn't reply to my texts. I was getting worried. Karen and Rollin told me the police have been here today. How are you?"

"It's complicated, Alexis."

He suddenly notices what I have in my hand. "Sarah! Please put that thing down."

"If I was going to do something stupid, it wouldn't be with this."

I shake the gun slightly in my hand and, without thinking, press a button on the grip. The cartridge clip is ejected and falls to the floor. A bullet rolls across the parquet.

Alexis can't help smiling. "You're right. As a solution, it'd probably be doomed to fail."

He picks up the bullet and the cartridge clip, gently takes the gun from my hand, and puts his arms around me as I cry. He says nothing until my breathing slows.

"This situation has knocked us all sideways. I don't know where I am either. We're discovering too many things, too quickly. That's why I keep my distance sometimes. I know that's not the image most people have of me. I guess it's a fear of being betrayed or disappointed, or both. It's hard to know who to trust."

I take a step back from him. He reaches out his hand and dries my cheeks, real tenderness in his eyes.

"I found the gun in his study, hidden in the ceiling vent. The police focused on the books, the drafts of manuscripts, the computer, the printer, but they missed this."

"You've got to hand it over to the police, Sarah. This is a serious weapon."

"Why did he even have it? A shotgun is one thing, but this . . . Do you think he felt threatened?"

"I don't know. His fans always struck me as mild-mannered people, no crazies among them. He never said or did anything controversial. Successful as he was, he was always discreet, wasn't he? He protected his own image and respected his readers and even his colleagues. At least I think so."

I'm starting to wonder if I knew Marceau only through what I read about him in glossy magazines or saw of him on TV shows. Was our whole relationship nothing but a clever script? This house a movie set? Where was the truth and where was the falsehood in our story?

Alexis puts his hands on my shoulders. "And did the police provide any answers?"

"They're doing their job. They have a few small leads. But I really don't get the impression they're making any progress."

"It's only the start. You can count on me, you know. I'm here for you. We're all going through a difficult time. If I can help you see things more clearly, it'll give me the feeling I'm doing something. We have to get back to some kind of normal life, at least for the sake of your kids."

He's right. Just getting back to ordinary life sounds great.

We step outside, the world draped in a veil of darkness. The air has grown cooler, laden with the scents of the surrounding woods. A breeze, as light as a sigh, rustles through the silvery leaves of the birches, mingling with the eternal lullaby of the lake. The moon, the pale queen, weaves a trail of light over the obsidian waters. And the Alps rise like sleeping giants, their peaks touching a sky studded with glittering stars. An eagle owl sings a solitary song, reminding me that night is never really silent for those who know how to listen. Beneath my feet, the grass is damp. Alexis opens the door of his car and switches on the headlights. The beams just about reach the dock. He leans inside and takes something out of the glove compartment.

"You know, I occasionally borrow a boat from your agency. Karen almost always lends me the same one, the one she has left when I ask her at the last minute. I have customers who sign on to almost anything I ask once I've taken them for a ride on the lake. It's a lucrative method."

We walk over to the landing stage. I haven't properly seen the object he's holding in his hand, but now he holds it out.

"It's what I thought," he said. "This is definitely from one of the pilings supporting your dock."

Quickly we both identify the piling that's missing its protective cover.

"I guess when a boat is badly tied up and the rope is removed too quickly, it's easy to dislodge this. It's a good thing it didn't end up in the water. Marceau and I went out lots of times from here, that's why I thought of it. What was this cover doing in the agency's boat? Isn't that boat too big to be tied up here?"

"It's an Antares Fly, more than thirty-five feet long and weighing nearly six and a half tons. Bringing it here would risk damaging things . . . No, it's just not possible."

We stand there, the silence broken only by the lapping of the lake under our feet. We're both puzzled. None of us use the agency's new boats for our private excursions, only the old boats that are no longer usable by customers. There is *no reason* the Antares Fly would have been at this dock.

~

As Alexis drives off in his Porsche, I continue to inspect the dock with the flashlight from my cell phone. I search for the slightest nick in the wood or paint. If you tied up in a hurry, you might possibly just throw a rope around one of the pilings. The old tires used as fenders certainly couldn't protect against a boat of that size.

I feel like I'm throwing questions into the deep waters of the lake without hope of an answer. I'm getting to the point where I doubt everything and everyone, reawakening anxieties I thought had long disappeared. Is it possible to recover from everything that haunts us?

I check the time on my phone. It's 11:15 p.m. I've forgotten all about the children. Without even bothering to lock up the house, I get into the pickup. But then a new thought occurs to me, and I set off for the agency. It won't take me too long. This business of the boat is nagging at me. Any clue that might help move this case forward is urgent, and I need a few moments alone at the office.

28

I park the pickup outside the agency, leaving the headlights on for a moment so I can count the boats. They're all there, bobbing slightly on the water, which is calm tonight. As soon as I get inside the office, I switch on my computer. While waiting for it to fire up, I consult the big spiral-bound diary Karen keeps. I notice she's slipped Delmas's business card between two of the pages. What was he looking for here? Karen told me he and his men had dropped by. Did they search the place the way they searched my house?

The connection log-in appears on the screen. I type out the password. It's rejected. I type it a second time. Rejected. My hands are starting to shake. I'm sure I've got the right password; I've been typing it without thinking for years. I keep trying. It just doesn't work. No matter, I can work without the booking schedule. There are only three boats to inspect. It's on one of them that Alexis found the piling covering from my old dock.

I grab the set of keys for the boats from the cupboard and the big battery-powered lantern. I make sure the lamp is working. It's used a lot, and there are always holds to light up and inventories to carry out in the boats our customers bring back to us: leaks, neglect, wear and tear . . .

Outside, from the dock, I light up the bows of the boats and the waterlines. Fish follow my beam of light, presumably hoping to find something to eat. On the forward part of one of the Antares Flys, I see something that wouldn't seem unusual to someone not looking for it. It's a mark beneath the level of the dock; it isn't surprising as the dock at home is lower than this one. There's no doubt: The edge of the bow has rubbed against the eroded black porous tires I fitted myself as makeshift fenders nearly ten years ago. I go on board and move the beam of light over the deck, the cabin, the rail, the cockpit. It's in perfect condition. It's less than five years old, which for a boat is almost brand new. This one and the other two were in for servicing just a few weeks ago. The man who did the work, Victor, is authorized by the manufacturer, and his business is located farther along the lake.

I unlock the cabin and go in, taking care on the steps. I hit the top of my forehead, and it's not the first time I've done that. It's sure to leave a nasty mark for several days. I sit on one of the banquettes and examine the entire cabin, then open all the chests, the storage in the banquettes, everything, top to bottom. But I don't see even the smallest mark, or anything even slightly suspicious. I slip into the tiny space that houses the inboard motor and lift a thin board that keeps the motor watertight. My flashlight lights up something vague, white, and shiny. As I pull it out, I see it's an opaque plastic bag, apparently hermetically sealed, that weighs at least two pounds. I feel my heart thumping in my chest. This bag has no business being here. All my senses are on the alert. What if this is the manuscript?

I shine the flashlight down and open the bag.

It's the odor that hits me first.

Marijuana. All kinds: dried leaves, bars of resin, gummies to be swallowed like candies, all in little sachets. In a flash, I remember what Karen said about my daughter: *Hermione is hiding joints in her room.* It's a good thing I'm the one who's come across this crap, not Karen. Or worse, the cops. And then it hits me. That good-for-nothing son of Victor, the boat repairer. He's sixteen and often does odd jobs for his father, and he likes hanging out with Hermione. Has he already taken her out for a ride on the lake to show off? I empty the rest of the bag, and what do I find? A box of condoms.

That little son of a bitch. She's twelve years old!

Sure, Hermione is almost a teenager, and she's starting to develop physically. But this? I grab the bag of pot and leave the cabin, banging my head again. In my anger and my pain, I kick the cockpit, but it doesn't calm me down. I empty the contents of the bag into the water. Some of it sinks immediately and some floats. I grab the boat hook from the rail and try to get the rest to sink, then move on to the second boat.

The same thing.

The little bastard is using our boats for his dirty work!

Soon afterward, I leave the dock with the empty plastic bags and the boxes of condoms. He's really well prepared, the little bastard—one box in each boat. I almost run to the office. With the scissors from the drawer next to the computer, I cut all the condoms into small pieces, find a large padded envelope, and stuff everything I've collected into it. I write the name of its young owner on it. I will only have one detour to make on the way to Karen's house. Time enough to leave this nice little package in front of the boy's door—or rather, his parents' door. He should understand the message.

Envelope in hand, I leave the agency, but something isn't right. The lights of my pickup are off. The landing stage and the boats are invisible in the darkness, and I can barely make out the truck. I can hear the slight lapping of the water on the hulls and the plaintive creaking of the boats against the landing stage as I move slowly to the truck and slip inside the door.

When I turn the key, the engine splutters and then starts.

So, the lights weren't off because the battery was down.

In the darkness, I feel a threat prowling around me, turning in concentric circles closer to me, holding its dirty hand out, ready to pounce on meat at a moment of its own choosing.

PART FOUR:

MURKY WATERS

29

Karen and Rollin live in a small house in Ballaison, surrounded by vines and wheat fields, about thirty miles from the lake. Given the house's slightly raised position, their living room has an unobstructed view over the lake. It was Alexis's contacts who helped them get a place in what was a very desirable new development about ten years ago.

The perfect house for a perfect Karen, who's looking after my children this evening.

And I was supposed to be there an hour ago, two hours ago . . . I've lost count.

I'm on the D225, approaching Massongy. My headlights sweep the cultivated fields, bend after bend. I'm following the markings on the road, as if hypnotized, when I hear strange noises coming from the back of the pickup. As if someone's knocking on the sheet metal. I can't see anything in the rearview mirror, just the red from my rear lights in the dark. My tires screech against the grassy edge of the narrow road. The pickup stops, and I get out with the engine still on, mosquitoes dancing in the beams of the headlights.

I walk around the vehicle and glance inside the bed. Light spilling from the ceiling of the cabin illuminates a large shiny-scaled fish lying there, motionless. It's a pike, nearly three feet long. Its gaping jaws look capable of easily killing its prey. But what's so strange and haunting is that its flesh is pierced with branches of all sizes, at least twenty of them, in no particular pattern. Like some kind of voodoo. A threatening message?

Next to the fish is something rectangular and brightly colored, which I recognize as the cover of one of Marceau's novels. I aim the flashlight of my cell phone on it. It's *The Lake Geneva Code*, which came out four years ago. The book is wet and swollen, completely misshapen. I pick it up carefully and the wet pages tear. It must have spent several days immersed in water to be in this state. I know this because once, a long time ago, when Marceau and I made love beside a pond, I dropped the book I was reading into the water. I completely forgot about it until I found it several days later, in the same state as this one.

Suddenly, the fish arches violently and its tail slaps on the metal. I scream, my heart pounding. Despite my disgust, I open the back of the truck, grab the end of the tail, and yank the fish out of the car. It plops down on the grass and rolls into the ditch, where it disappears.

Someone was there. Why? To spy on me, to threaten me? Like those nights when I go out in the garden? Is this real, or am I going crazy?

I close the back of the truck and set off again. On the way out of Massongy, I stop to deposit my package of torn condoms outside the little bastard's door. I never want to see him again, not around my boats and not around Hermione.

It's after midnight by the time I get to Karen's house. The lights are on, and I see Karen's silhouette behind the bay window. She's waiting for me in the doorway, then comes out and shuts the door gently behind her, isolating the two of us for a moment in the soft coolness of the night.

"You're late, Sarah. I was getting worried." She tilts her head to the side. "What's going on? The children can stay here if you like. I've been letting them play computer games. It's the only thing that cheers them up."

Karen's looking me up and down now. I pass my hand over my forehead, but it's a wasted effort.

"Did you hurt yourself?"

"It's nothing, I was on one of the boats and I stupidly banged my head."

"At this time of night? What were you doing out there?"

"I needed to check the booking schedule, but I couldn't connect to the computer. Have you changed the password? And what about Captain Delmas? What did the two of you talk about in the agency?"

This time, I'm the one staring at her.

She's silent for a moment before replying. "Are you sure everything's all right, Sarah? I didn't change the password; it's been the same ever since we opened the agency. I would have told you if I had!"

The song of the crickets in the nearby field is louder than before. There's no point in my mentioning the voodoo fish or the disintegrating book. It would be a reason not to leave with the children. Nor am I going to mention the marijuana. Best to get to the point.

"I'm taking Hermione and Benjamin home. We need to spend time together . . . and talk."

Before letting me in, Karen again gives me a solemn look. She seems to be hesitating about what she has to say to me.

"Captain Delmas did come to see me. He asked me questions about Marceau, about you, and about the children. I didn't tell him anything important. You and I know there are things that don't need to come out."

"Things that have nothing to do with Marceau's death don't need to be brought up," I reply, more curtly than I intended. "I know what we risk, I know we could lose the agency. And Delmas isn't interested in any deals we might have made to buy and sell boats."

From the way she frowns, I sense how anxious Karen is. "We agree about that," she says. "We had no choice. It was that or bankruptcy. Although I still don't understand why you didn't want to ask Marceau for help when it happened. I hope it wasn't pride. As for the story of the children with the caps and the robbery at the Forest Center, Delmas asked about that. He questioned Zoé. All she did was give him some of those caps advertising Rollin's food truck—we have dozens of them in the house—in exchange for a handful of candies recovered at the time of the robbery. But Zoé didn't steal anything! And anyway, two kids have been identified and questioned, end of story."

"What do you mean, end of story?"

"Don't mix up our children in all this, do you understand? They have nothing to do with it, and you know that. Delmas got in touch again about the robbery. The two kids spilled the beans. They'd sold some of the stolen equipment on eBay. He asked them about the sling, but the kids didn't know anything about that. Anyway, it had nothing to do with Zoé."

I've pushed my way into the house. Hermione and Benjamin are both ready. Did they hear our conversation? Hermione walks past me without a kiss, or even a word, and heads for the pickup. Once there, she turns.

"I'm tired, I want to go home."

Benjamin, at least, is polite and kisses Karen. "G-goodnight, Karen."

I sense that something is wrong. I try to create a diversion.

"Isn't Rollin here?"

"He's repairing a leak in his food truck. He's been in the garage for ages. I guess that's his way of getting through things right now, disappearing into the garage."

It's only once we're in the pickup that Hermione finally opens up and my doubts disappear.

"You should tell Karen to stop asking us all those stupid questions. The cops are bad enough."

"Sh-she's w-worried about us, and sh-she's right," Benjamin says calmly. I'm surprised. Has he matured without my realizing it? I start the engine, but I don't immediately reverse. My hands cling to the wheel.

"Wait for me a second. Don't move, OK?"

My tone seems to surprise them. I switch off the engine, get out, and head straight for the garage. A ray of light filters beneath the shutter, which isn't completely closed. I hear muffled voices from a radio. Rollin has his head in the engine. Above the static from the radio, I hear him sniffing. I imagine him drying his cheeks with a cloth covered in oil and grease.

"Leave me alone. Go back to the kids. There's nothing more to say than what we told the police."

"And what did you tell the police?"

Rollin looks up in surprise, banging his head on the hood. He was expecting to see Karen. I don't feel sorry for him. I'm ready to bring the hood down on his neck unless he tells me what they told the police.

"Sarah? You should have told me you were here. Karen's with the kids."

"Don't bullshit me, let's talk about the police! What did you tell them?"

His cheeks turn red. "Listen . . . They bombarded us with questions, first about Marceau, then about the children, and then about you. Karen had to tell them that you weren't at the agency the day Marceau died. She didn't know where you were. She tried to cover for you, but Delmas put pressure on her."

I feel my heart beating loudly in my chest and heat rising to my face. My husband's death, all my friendships collapsing, Reynaud, Karen . . . I give a violent kick to a container full of black oil. The liquid spurts everywhere, over the food truck, the workbench, and the adjacent wall. But most of it spreads in a viscous mass across the floor, like the mark of a betrayal it'll be difficult to eradicate. I leave the shutter wide open when I leave. There's nothing more to hide now. Poor Rollin is silhouetted against the light of the garage. He's been unmasked, forced out of his hole. I know he, too, is suffering. But tonight, I need to feel pain in others. Just to know that I'm not the only one.

30

I'll never forget the faces of Hermione and Benjamin through the windows of the pickup. They witnessed the whole scene. When I get back in the truck, they don't ask me any questions. My anger pulses. I'm radioactive. I drive; they keep silent. The headlights slice through the darkness.

Nothing is happening the way it should.

Given the state of my nerves right now, it's best for me to avoid sensitive subjects. But sooner or later, there are abscesses I'm going to have to lance. They say everything looks better in the morning. But what if you can't sleep and the night has brought you nothing but nightmares?

We get home. While the children get ready for bed, I go back outside and look around. All I see in the dark are moving shadows. This is becoming a ritual, but I can't shrug off the feeling that an evil presence is tirelessly prowling. According to the doctor, paranoia is common after a shock. I take my suspicions with me when I walk back into the house. Hermione has already locked herself in her room. I kiss Benjamin on his forehead and stroke his hair before he slips out of my reach.

"G-goodnight. M-mom."

I leave his door ajar. After his father's death and all we're going through, I hope there is a remnant of his childhood self left, that all of this hasn't destroyed it. The anger that's been burning inside me for hours suddenly rises to my throat. I rush to the bathroom and look for the bottles of pills the doctor prescribed. There are lots of them. Clearly, I haven't followed the treatment very well. I put together something to help me sleep and calm my anxiety, a cocktail of benzodiazepine, zolpidem, and Xanax. Maybe not the best drugs to mix, but at least I don't add alcohol. I lie down on the bed, which I haven't made for days. A numbness overcomes me almost immediately, anesthetizing me. I no longer have the strength to get up and undress. Sleep comes soon enough, although I know the nightmares will be back in three hours. These three hours are the only respite I'm going to get.

Vertigo again, and the fall into the abyss with Marceau. My heart explodes, my hands are moist, I sit up abruptly. My head is spinning. I look at the alarm. 4:42 a.m. I'm stifling. I get out of bed, swaying slightly, holding myself on the doorframe, on the walls. I need air, so I go outside again. The sky is filled with stars, though the first light of day is just visible. I'm in a total brain fog, floating between two worlds. I walk across the lawn toward the woods. A glimmer amid the trees attracts my attention like the beam of a flashlight dancing between the branches. I know these woods well. I sometimes come here to look for kindling. I hear whispering, and it sounds like a child. Benjamin and Hermione sometimes play here, hiding behind the tree trunks. I go further into the woods, following the whispering, which I have to convince myself is not my imagination. I think I hear the word *Mom*. My senses go on high alert. I can hardly see anything. Then there's a cracking sound, and my anxiety turns to fear. I do a U-turn and stop dead. A few yards away, a motionless figure is standing next to a tree. Or maybe two. Animals? There are deer at this time of year, sometimes boars. I'm breathing hard. I break into a run, and my left foot catches on a root. I stumble and fall forward, my right knee slamming down on something hard. I feel a searing pain, but before I can cry out, my head hits the trunk of a tree. There's a flash in my eyes; then everything goes black.

~

I come to. I must have lost consciousness for a few seconds, I think. The fear resurfaces immediately. I get to my feet. I look around for the figures, but there is nothing there. I turn around, and then I see a small moving shape that looks like a child, some three feet from a large oak.

"Benjamin!"

There's no reaction. I take a closer look, sudden terror hollowing my stomach. The shape has no legs, and it seems to be suspended from the oak. This time I empty my lungs. The blood rises to my face as I scream.

"Benjamin!!!"

I rush to the shape and take it in my arms, but it deflates like a burst balloon. The noise of tearing.

In my hands, an overcoat belonging to Benjamin, the hood hooked over a branch. I can barely breathe; I feel like I'm about to faint. Suddenly, as if I've only just become aware of it, it strikes me that I'm in the woods, while the children are alone in the house. I have to get back to them, protect them, make sure they're safe in their beds.

I run as I've never run before, falling several times. I see lights in the house, too many for a normal night. A car is parked outside the house. I run some more. Benjamin is outside, standing next to a man. It's Reynaud.

"Where were you, Sarah? What were you doing in the woods?"

All I can think of is to hug my son. I want him in my arms, to breathe him in deeply.

"B-but is that my c-coat?"

I realize I'm still holding it.

Hermione approaches and joins in the hug. It's been a long time. Reynaud also takes a step forward. I put out my arm to stop him. I'm ready to bite, to kill.

"Sarah . . ."

"Don't come any closer!"

"Benjamin called me. He told me he saw you go into the woods. I came as fast as I could. Sarah . . . we have to talk."

"Not here, not now!"

Reynaud shakes his head sadly. He takes an envelope from his pocket and gives it to me. "I would have liked to always be there for her . . . Just like I'm here for you tonight. I only want to help you, Sarah."

Then he waves at the children and turns to go. I watch him leave, totally lost. I kiss the children again and ask them to go back inside. "I'll join you in a minute."

I open the envelope and discover a photograph of Jade, smiling radiantly at the camera. On the back, in her handwriting: *With you forever.* She really loved him. Yves Reynaud. I don't understand anything anymore.

The children are in the living room, standing side by side. They don't seem to know what to do with themselves. My heart contracts.

"What were you doing in the woods, Mom?"

The reality of the moment catches up with me. With Benjamin's question still floating in the air, it's the look that Hermione gives me that hurts the most. A dismayed look at what I've become. My shoes covered in mud, my clothes dirty too, the scratches on my arms, the bruises. My nocturnal wanderings, my unstable behavior. I see in that look something between disgust and shame. I bite my cheeks, incapable of hiding.

"You know what my school friends are saying? That they're only investigating because of the money. Because the insurance won't pay out for a mountaineering accident if the safety rules haven't been followed."

"Are you sure they're really your friends, Hermione?"

It's not a very kind answer, but it's all I'm capable of.

"Oh, because you know all about friends, do you? Like Karen, who suspects us and thinks we're a bad influence on Zoé?"

"Karen is . . . worried. And with good reason. The little idiot you hang out with hid dope in the agency's boats! I don't want you to see him anymore, is that understood?"

"I'm not going back to school anyway!"

With this last cry, Hermione goes up to her room.

Was everything about to spin out of control even before Marceau died? What's more terrifying than this momentary loss of control is the thought that I may never get it back. The only way I can save my children and give my life some meaning is by finding out what's behind all the tragedies that have been pursuing us for twenty years. Everything is linked, one way or another. I'm convinced of it.

31

The garden is shrouded in early-dawn mist.

I couldn't get back to sleep. Instead, I've been wandering between the house and the garden. I don't know exactly what time it is when I pass the hangar, still wide open just as Marceau left it. The grass is growing in the vast meadow where he took off and landed. I approach the plane, run my hand over the propeller, then over the side of the engine. A mechanical smell, a mixture of oil and gasoline, floats around me. Marceau loved that smell, loved having it on him. I sometimes caught him sniffing his jacket the same way he deeply inhaled the air of the lake or the mountains.

I close my eyes. *Why did you go? How could you be so selfish? Did you even think about our children?*

My phone emits a beep. A text.

> Sarah, did you change the password of the agency computer? You mentioned it last night, I can't connect. Karen.

Even when I'm not at the agency, I cause problems.

I thought it was you. I couldn't connect last night either.

I'm not crazy; I didn't change the password. Only Karen and I use it. The little dots disappear, no message. She doesn't believe me. She thinks I'm cracking up. Then another text.

I'll call the computer repair people. It's weird.

I feel like saying it's got nothing to do with me, but that would be another way of calling my sanity into question. I have the feeling an invisible hand is manipulating me. Who could it be? I stopped the medication a few days after Marceau died. That crap was burning my brain. But am I making up everything that's happening to me?

Suddenly, I hear the horn of the pickup. The old clock reads 7:44 a.m. I should have left for school with the children fifteen minutes ago. I rush out of the hangar and see Benjamin sitting in the passenger seat, leaning over the wheel. A second shrill blast of the horn reaches me like a slap—a reprimand by my own children.

The engine is already on; Benjamin started it before I got there. He knows I don't like him doing that, but I'm not going to tell him off today. Benjamin replies before I ask the question.

"Her-Hermione already left. Sh-she's w-walking."

I bite my lower lip. What a bad mother I am! I drive fast, hoping to make up time. Hermione has almost walked a couple of miles by the time I spot her. She turns, grim faced. I slow down as I come next to her, but she keeps walking. Benjamin lowers his window.

"Hermione, get in," I say. "There's still a half mile to go. We're late."

She doesn't look at me but continues on her way, walking even faster. Then, as I continue to follow her, she turns toward me.

"*You're* late! Roll up the window, Benjamin!"

End of discussion. I speed up again, heading in the direction of Yvoire. I watch her disappear in my rearview mirror.

~

Benjamin waves goodbye to me before walking through the school gate. He walks past a little group, some of whom I recognize as friends from his birthday party at the house three months ago. Only one of them turns as he passes, and only for a brief moment. Benjamin sits down on the steps of the school, alone. Seeing me still parked on the sidewalk, he lowers his head and opens his satchel. He takes out the snack I made him. An awkward-looking young boy joins him. A new friend, maybe. I'm so tired, and seeing him like this makes me sad. I hope I'll be strong enough to talk to him tonight. I need to tell him that things will get better. We'll make it through this.

The agency is close to Benjamin's school, so that's where I head. Before I get very far, I see two motorcycles right behind me. One of them suddenly accelerates and comes next me, the passenger aiming and snapping away with a huge camera lens at me. I think I've finally thrown it off, but when I get to the agency, the parking lot is swarming with reporters. Karen waves her arms at me from the dock, and more than a dozen reporters do a U-turn. I quickly veer into the adjacent street. My tires screech, and I smash my side-view mirror against a TV truck with a satellite dish on top. I have the feeling I'm in the middle of a bad 1980s cop show. Now two more motorcycles are after me. Five yards farther on, I hurtle into a deserted parking lot and cross it without stopping. At the other end is a forest path where I often jog, a minefield of fallen branches and potholes. The pickup bounces up and down, and I bang my head twice on the ceiling of the cabin, but the vultures are no longer behind me. I get back on the road less than half a mile farther on, car horns blasting furiously at me. I switch on the car radio. Whatever station I try, the "Marceau Miller case" is all anybody's talking about. On one station, the reporter goes to a special correspondent who's at the scene.

"I'm waiting in a conference room in the town hall of Thonon-les-Bains, along with about thirty other journalists, for a press conference by the mayor and Captain Robin Delmas, who's in charge of the investigation. It's crowded, and I'm fortunate to have been able to get into the conference room, which has now been closed for security reasons. Many of my colleagues are stuck outside. More than a hundred fans of the late author have also gathered in the town, and the local authorities are having difficulty containing the outpouring of attention. Everyone's demanding to know the truth about what they're calling the Marceau Miller case. We all hope this press conference will throw some light on the progress of the investigation. The mayor is now taking his place at the microphone. Captain Delmas is standing next to him."

I'm about to hear my life laid out for everyone to talk about. I squeeze the steering wheel. I already feel disgust and anger rising inside me, powerless to do anything about what's about to happen. I always expect the worst, and I'm seldom disappointed. As announced, it's the mayor who speaks first. I remember that he complained to his counterpart in Yvoire when Karen and I planned to open our agency, arguments that were questionable legally. The local boat renters' mafia clearly had him, and maybe still has him. At that time, Marceau used his contacts to get things moving. God knows what other pressures the mayor is under, especially with the investigation being led by that idiot Delmas.

"I want first of all to express the feelings of sadness we all share. The reasons behind the tragedy that has occurred in our area need to be explored, which is why I ask all our citizens to let Captain Delmas and his team do their work. This case, which has now captured the attention of the media, needs to be handled calmly and without extraneous problems getting in the way of their investigation. I'd like to ask the public to respect the process unfolding behind the scenes. We do not wish to tarnish the memory of Marceau Miller or add to the distress his family and close friends are already experiencing."

"Monsieur Mayor, is it true that you authorized climbing on the rock face where Marceau Miller died, even though it's a place that doesn't meet safety standards?"

"I don't know where you got that information, but it's false."

"Another question, Monsieur Mayor. You were also mayor when another tragedy struck the Miller family twenty years ago. Is there a connection between the disappearance of Jade Miller, the writer's sister, and his death?"

"Could tensions within the Miller marriage be behind this tragedy?"

"Is it true that Miller left his wife and children an enormous fortune?"

Is this what it feels like to be dragged publicly through the mud? Benjamin and Hermione are going to have to face all this crap. They'll be bombarded with questions and hasty judgments, whether by other kids at school or by their parents. I'm tempted to turn off the radio, but I want to know what they're saying. It's harder to fight when you don't know what the monster looks like. I'm not going to get out of this mess by blindfolding myself.

Captain Delmas starts speaking, his tone unbearable to me.

"The investigation is ongoing, and as I'm sure you'll appreciate, some things have to remain confidential. All the same, there's enough evidence to point to homicide as the cause of death. We're taking great pains not to jump to obvious conclusions, which is why we're making careful progress."

That son of a bitch!

"We are deploying all the means at our disposal as we reconstruct exactly what happened. We're currently questioning the victim's friends and family, checking everyone's alibi. Everything relating in any way to Marceau Miller's activities over the last months and years is being examined. The writer's computer equipment has been sequestered, and our specialists are at work. Crucial testimonies have been taken into account, suggesting new avenues of inquiry. No lead is being ruled out at the present moment."

"Captain Delmas, do you think you can find answers where your predecessor, Yves Reynaud, didn't find any for Jade Miller?"

"We're not allowing our investigation to be influenced by anyone or anything."

"Captain Delmas, a climbing sling from the Forest Center is said to have been found near the place where the writer died. There was a robbery at the center some time ago, committed by a gang of children, including,

we believe, the Miller children. As in eighty percent of solved cases, do you think the answer is to be found within the Miller family?"

"The robbery has nothing to do with this case. We found some of the stolen gear at the bottom of the harbor in Yvoire. It was thrown there by two young men on scooters, who were identified by a witness. Both have now confessed. The Miller children are not involved at this stage."

This time it's the brake I crush with my foot. The tires leave two black skid marks on the rough asphalt. I lean over the ditch with a painful cramp that brings tears to my eyes. A trickle of bile rises to my lips, but I'm so angry I can't even throw up.

32

For about half an hour, I've been walking in circles around the house. I need to chill. Maybe I should go running. I put on a T-shirt and leggings. A call interrupts my preparations. What's the point of answering when the only thing I'd like to be told is that Marceau is coming back? But the name of Louise's care home appears on my screen. They never call.

"Hello, Madame Miller. It's about your grandmother."

"I'm listening," I say, my throat tight.

"Following an incident, your grandmother had a dizzy spell. She's come to, but we're keeping an eye on her."

"What kind of incident?"

"In connection with her diaries. She couldn't find a few of them, and she's convinced someone stole them. It's not uncommon with Alzheimer's patients. And in her case, the disease is getting worse."

"OK, I'll be right there! I want to see her."

As I drive, I can't get out of my mind that this kind of reaction is not like her. Of course, I find it difficult to look reality in the face when it comes to my grandmother. I have a tendency to deny how much the disease is affecting her.

When I get to the care home, the nurse who takes care of Louise is waiting for me.

"Your grandmother is still weak, and very shaken, but her appetite's fine and . . . well, you know her, she has an iron will."

"And what happened with the diaries?"

"It happened late morning. A colleague was bringing Granny Louise her medication and found her unconscious in her room. When she came to, she got very upset about the notebooks. They weren't in her chest of drawers anymore, she said. But she misplaces lots of things, you know."

"Never her diaries," I said.

"We calmed her by bringing her notebooks from last year. She has so many that we put some aside, once or twice a year, to avoid her getting confused. She fills one a week, sometimes more."

"And which notebooks are missing?"

"It's the ones from March to May this year."

When we come to the door of Louise's room, I ask the nurse to leave me alone with her for a while. I wait until she walks away before I knock at the door. My grandmother greets me with her disarming smile. The nurse was right: She does look more tired, but I'm just as tired. In her arms, I find the warmth I need. We embrace for several minutes without talking. We don't need to, this long embrace is enough, but our respite is short-lived.

"They stole my diaries, you know! Don't go thinking I'm batty. But they didn't get these!"

Her face lights up as she takes the books from the last few weeks out from underneath where she is sitting. With her real memory fading, these books *are* her memory. Depriving her of them is the worst thing you could do to her.

"Can I see them, Louise?"

She looks at the covers, gently strokes them, then hands the books to me. "I don't usually show them to anyone. They're quite private, but I trust you. You're the only one I trust these days. Even here, I have to be careful."

I go back to the pages preceding Marceau's death. It's like going back in time. Since Louise is precise and well organized, I soon find the page relating to Marceau's last visit. It was the day after he went to the bank and took his manuscript out of the safety-deposit box.

Friday, April 23, 2021, 11:02 a.m. Visit from Marceau. Today, it was Marceau who went with me on my morning walk. We talked about the manuscript. Marceau is a great writer. He's married to my darling granddaughter, Sarah. They've given me two great-grandchildren, Hermione and Benjamin.

As I read, I'm moved by what it must be like to have to write things down in order to remember them, even the most important things, such as the names of the people you love. I continue, my eyes getting misty.

"Why is everyone so interested in my diaries all of a sudden? I know Marceau has left us. I think a lot about you and the children. In the newspapers, they say it might not have been an accident. I collect all the articles I can find. I tear out the pages when the guard dogs aren't looking."

I wipe away a tear as discreetly as possible. Her memory may be slipping, but not her intelligence.

"Marceau mentioned a manuscript. That's what I'm looking for."

"Then keep reading. My diaries know more about it than I do. And take the others out too. They brought me the ones from last year. I'm not stupid—I saw what they were doing."

I continue reading while she takes the other notebooks from her chest of drawers.

It's his most important manuscript. This year he added a chapter and went over some of them. He's been doing that every year since Jade disappeared. He thanks me for what I tell him about his little sister, or at least what I'm able to remember from time to time. Sometimes, I'd like to make things up, like a writer, so that

Marceau will stay with me a while longer. He's so kind. With his voice and his words, I can understand how my Sarah had a crush on him. He talks to me about the lake, the mountains, and the forests. All of that is in his manuscript. And other things too, very personal things. But he made me promise never to tell anyone. I'm keeping my word. In my day, promises meant something. Today, everything's going to hell. Like my damned head.

I don't find anything else, so I pick up another, in which she's highlighted the pages that mention Marceau's visits. The only references to the manuscript I can find are superficial. Marceau was on his guard—I sense that. Did he need to confide in someone all the same? What's clear is that he revised the manuscript every year. And especially when a new novel was about to appear. It was like a ritual.

"Do you have the diary from April last year, just before his novel was published?"

"Yes, and I even have one from two years ago, 2019, around the same period. It's almost my oldest. That was when I got the idea for the diaries. A good idea from a crazy head, I guess."

As I get ready to read the diary from May 2020, the nurse arrives. "Did you call me?"

I frown, but Louise winks at me—she pressed her emergency remote.

"Could you bring me my notebook from April 2019, please? Thank you very much."

I smile and take her hand.

"You have to hassle them a little. That way they know I'm still here."

I press her hand to my cheek. With her other hand, she motions me to continue reading.

In 2020, on Tuesday, April 28, Marceau was only able to phone her. It was during the first COVID lockdown, and visits weren't allowed. It was a terrible year for writers and publishers—that was all she had preserved from their conversation. It makes me dizzy to see how, in her writing and her way of telling things, her cognitive state seems less affected.

The nurse arrives with the diary from April 2019. She is followed by a doctor, who motions me over and asks me in a low voice to cut the visit short. I've already spent a lot of time with her, he says. I mustn't tire her out.

I take the exercise book the nurse is holding. "I'm borrowing this one! It'll be a good excuse to come and see you again in a few days!"

"Make good use of it," Louise says with a quick glance at the nurse and the doctor. "At least I know that one's in good hands."

On the way out, I stop for a few moments on the front steps and look at my cell phone. I can't continue all alone; I need help. I'm too lost, too tired. But who to call? Reynaud is the first person who comes to mind. I try to dismiss him from my thoughts, try to think of someone else. But, despite the fear I felt—and still feel—because of that moment in his cellar, it's his face that keeps coming back to me. He's my one recourse, the man who's always been there for me. I can't forget the shock of discovering his relationship with Jade—the age difference, all the questions still unanswered—but Marceau trusted him. And who else can I call?

He picks up immediately. From his voice, I sense how happy he is to hear from me. How relieved too. I tell him about the missing diaries.

"I'll deal with the care home, Sarah. I can check on everyone who came and went on the day your grandmother's diaries were stolen. I'm more qualified for that than Delmas. That's the advantage of age: I know a lot of people here. I'll be able to spot who's a familiar face and who's a stranger to the area."

I thank him and walk to the pickup. Before I start the engine, I open the notebook to April 2019.

Thursday, April 18, 2019, 10:40 a.m. Visit from Marceau. Today is Saint Perfectus's day, so it's only natural I should get a visit from the most famous writer in the country. I'm so proud of him. His new book will be out soon. They're already talking about it in the press. Marceau even brought me an advance copy of an interview that will appear in a top magazine. He's in his element, and the photograph of him is superb, as usual.

[. . .] He needed information for that very important manuscript of his. We went over old memories, those of his teenage years, when Jade was still with us. I had so much pleasure reliving them. Marceau confirmed that, like every year, when he has finished his revisions, he'll put a new version of his manuscript in the safety-deposit box at the bank. And out of superstition or some wild idea, he also puts a new copy in the place where the story began. As he said: "The work of a writer, Louise, consists of constantly rewriting. The more secrets a story contains, the more demanding it is."

Nothing else.

No location mentioned. Not a single clue.

But now I know for certain that there is, or was, a copy of the manuscript.

33

KAREN

A white van has parked by the dock. No logo indicating press or TV, and it's only 8:35 a.m.—a bit early for reporters.

I've been waiting for him. Without access to the computer, it's been hell at the agency, and I have no intention of doing twice the work to keep up with things.

"It's good to see you. I was wondering if you were going to come."

"Thank you, Madame Uldry. Karen, isn't it? We're rarely received with so much enthusiasm."

I look at him. He doesn't seem to have brought any equipment.

"You are from Lake Geneva Computer Assistance, aren't you?"

"I work for the newspaper *Le Messager*. I cover Chablais and Faucigny."

My enthusiasm fades.

"Get out!"

"I'll be quick! Just two or three questions."

"I warn you, I will throw you in the lake if you continue. Just get the hell out! I've already taken enough shit from reporters like you. And since you're the last to arrive, I guess that means you're the worst."

The idiot gets back in his van. I can hardly imagine the hell Sarah must be going through, being hounded like this. Still no answer to my text. Looking up, I see the weather forecast wasn't lying. I hurry inside as the sky darkens. A storm is brewing, and the emergency weather service says it's going to be a big one. I grab the radio microphone and switch to channel twelve. I'm not taking any risks. Only a few thrill seekers have rented boats today, but now things are turning dangerous.

"This is a safety announcement," I say into the microphone. "Please return to harbor immediately. The weather conditions are no longer favorable for sailing. Gusts of more than forty knots are expected, with a strong swell in the shallows and very poor visibility. I repeat, this is a safety announcement. Please return immediately to shore."

As I put the microphone down, as if to prove my point, the rain starts. Wind sweeps across the lake. The sky gets black as coal, and in a few minutes, the rain is coming down in sheets. I should have made the emergency call sooner, but I've been so preoccupied. A drumming sound makes me jump. It's the computer repair guy beating on the window. He's wearing a hat with the company logo on it, so no chance of getting it wrong this time.

The man comes in, soaked even after walking a few yards from his van. "Good morning, madame, nasty weather for sailing today!"

"Nasty weather period. Here, follow me. It's the password. It doesn't work anymore."

"No worries, I'll fix it."

He sits down and seems relaxed, as if everything has already been solved. He puts his soaked hat on the corner of the desk, and it drips onto my handbag, which I wipe with a tissue.

"Sorry about that, madame. I try to keep wet things away from the machine."

Without wasting a moment, he gets down to work. He's clearly in his element.

"You're right, madame, the password isn't being recognized. Have you tried everything?"

Does he think I'm stupid? From my expression, he knows I'm not amused. He gets down on his knees and crawls under the desk. I can hear him tinkering. When he comes back out, he's got a smug look on his face.

"Do you still need me?" I ask. "I've left you the boxes with the DVDs and everything that came with the equipment. Please, I don't want to lose any of my data."

"It'll be fine, madame, and it'll be quick. I'll reboot it in safe mode and check for malware."

"If you say so. Would you like a coffee? The agency's coffee is pretty good."

He smiles, brandishing a can of Red Bull he's taken out of his bag. I wait in an armchair, as if I were a customer at my own agency. The weather has gotten even worse, and none of the three boats that are out have returned yet. I know the storm is settling in because the roof on the west side of the agency starts whistling, a bad sign.

"There you are, Madame Uldry, all fixed."

"Already?"

"I put M@rVeL42 as a temporary password. Marvel like the comics: capital *M*, the 'at' symbol instead of the *a*, and every other letter after that a capital. You can never be too careful."

His smile is annoyingly triumphant. At the same time, it's my first good news of the day.

"Before you leave, can I ask you a simple question? How can a password change if nobody changes it?"

He has the smile of a naughty child.

"I checked the logs and the system event."

I don't understand any of this gobbledygook, but I really don't want him to go into a long explanation.

"And?"

"The message is clear, madame. Someone did change the password. I can even tell you exactly when. The day before yesterday, at precisely 12:28 p.m."

Right in the middle of my lunch break.

"There's your answer, and if there were just two of you in the office at that time, you know who to speak to."

"Sarah wasn't here the day before yesterday at that time," I say, thinking out loud, forgetting the man is even there.

"I'm no cop," he says, "but machines don't lie."

I turn to the lake, worried about the safety of our customers still out on the water. In my mind, I'm still going over details the cops are sure to dig into sooner or later.

"Tell me, Madame Uldry: Does this have anything to do with what they're talking about on the radio? I mean, about that writer. His wife is your colleague, isn't she?"

"Have a good day," I say.

That writer . . . Once he's left, I walk over to the row of Marceau's novels on the shelf. I run my hand over the spines. Not a trace of dust, as if he's still here, as if everything is normal.

I grab my binoculars. Visibility is bad, but I spot the three boats following each other like ducklings, buffeted by the wind. I breathe a sigh of relief, put on my yellow oilskin jacket, and hurry to the dock to guide them in. It won't be easy with this wind blowing so hard, but I hope to avoid as much damage to the boats as possible. No sooner have I set foot on the dock, which is being pummeled from all directions, than the first boat arrives.

"Slow down!" I scream into the wind. "Slow down, for Christ's sake!"

The bow of the first boat is already scraping the metal rail of the landing, just next to the fenders, making a horrendous noise. I grab the end of the mooring rope, which is flying in the wind, and almost fall into the water. The second boat hits the first one with a thud, then quickly reverses, only to knock into the third.

"No! Moor on the other side!"

The wind keeps slamming the boats into each other. Once the first has been secured, the customer who hired it, and who's more skillful than the other two, gives me a hand.

"Thank God we have insurance, gentlemen!!"

I prefer not to do the tally now, but there are bound to be expenses, not to mention the damage to the dock. Annoyed, I motion them to come inside the office while I make sure the boats are secure. It's only now that I notice that one of the boats that's usually moored here is missing. There's no loose rope to indicate that someone has gone out, and I can't see anything drifting on the lake or washed up on a nearby shore. Still lashed by the wind, I almost have to double over to walk back to the office.

I get out of my soaked oilskin. The men are a lot less talkative than they were this morning. I give them the papers they'll need to show the insurance company, which they sign before they leave, not looking very happy. It means a lot of extra paperwork for me, but my main concern right now is the missing boat. It doesn't make any sense. I suddenly think to check the keys, and the set for the missing boat is gone. Cell service is bad due to the storm. Maybe an antenna has been damaged. It wouldn't be the first time. I send a text instead.

> Sarah, I asked the customers who were out on the lake to come back in due to the storm, but a boat is still missing. Did you borrow it?

The wind blows the door open, and the pamphlets on the counter fly off in all directions. I turn and am shocked to see Captain Robin Delmas and a member of his team standing on the welcome mat.

"We're looking for your husband, Monsieur Rollin Uldry. Would you know where we can find him?"

He certainly doesn't bother too much about being polite. I'm starting to understand why Sarah finds him so insufferable.

"He's probably gone home, given the storm. What do you want with him?"

"We have some questions for him—some things don't quite add

up. Maybe you can help us. For example, how's his business doing? You must know, surely?"

I don't like his question at all, let alone the discreet but thorough search of the agency his colleague is quietly undertaking.

"I don't know what you're looking for, but we both provide for our family. That way, when times are tough for one of us, things balance out."

"In other words, it's a good thing you have your business. That's what we thought, but it seems he's found other ways to make ends meet. The strange thing is that he uses his truck instead of finding another vehicle, which isn't very smart of him."

I put my hand slowly down on the desk, as if to support myself.

"What are you talking about? Do you mind explaining?"

"Let's just say he's been making deliveries that don't have much to do with sandwiches. Marijuana and so on. A nice little side job."

I think about those long periods when Rollin shuts himself up in the garage. Have things been that bad? Couldn't he have found something else to help keep his business going? I don't even know what to say to the cops.

"You seem as surprised as we are," Delmas continues. "Do you think your husband is hiding anything else? Has anything unusual happened lately that you want to tell us about? If you have any details, now's the time to share them with us. You'd be helping him, and it's always worse when we discover it later."

Suddenly, I realize there's no way to fight.

"What do you want me to say? Nothing is normal anymore. The idea of my husband running a business at all is quite amazing. Of course, I'd prefer if he'd stuck with lettuce and tomatoes."

Even Delmas feels sorry for me.

"When there's a murder, we have to dig into everything, and sometimes what we dig up isn't pretty. We're just doing our job."

I close my eyes for a second, just long enough for a short, naive prayer that this nightmare does not touch Zoé. Delmas knocks twice on the counter. The officer who is still rummaging about the agency joins him, and at last they leave.

On my phone, a reply from Sarah.

> I had the boats tagged two months ago, and it's on the lake apparently. I'm going to look for it.

34

My tires skid on the muddy path leading to Reynaud's. Rain lashes the truck in waves, and my headlights can barely penetrate it. It's only noon, but it's as dark as nightfall. I realize I'm at the house, and the pickup slides to a halt. I'm not at all dressed for this weather, and the rain immediately soaks my hair, my clothes. Reynaud is waiting for me at the door.

"What terrible weather, Sarah! I'm afraid I haven't found anything, even though I checked everyone entering and leaving your grandmother's care home. I have no idea who could have stolen her diaries."

The gentleness of his voice does me a lot of good. I wonder how I could have doubted our good old Reynaud for one second, even after the shock of discovering his relationship with Jade. I shouldn't have gotten so hysterical. I can see how worried he still is about me. Water is streaming down my face. I push back my wet hair.

The best defense is attack. "The diaries aren't the most urgent thing right now. Is your boat ready? Is the tank full?"

"What do you want with my boat, Sarah? You're not going anywhere in this weather! Are you crazy or what?"

"One of the agency's boats is out in the middle of the lake."

"You mean one of your customers didn't get back in time? We have to call the emergency services. I have the number right here."

I stop him.

"No, it's not a customer."

"Wait, I don't understand. What do you mean?"

Right now, I don't even know what I'm thinking. "I've had more than enough of always being one step behind. Someone's trying to drive me crazy."

"I don't know what you've got in mind, Sarah. But whatever it is, going out in this weather means certain death."

I take a deep breath and tell him everything. After all, he's the only person I really trust. "First of all, the money in the bank but no manuscript. The surveillance footage. Climbing gear where you least expect it. Suspicious traces in the place where Marceau died. A gun hidden in the ceiling of his study. IT equipment disappearing. Passwords that change by themselves. A fish thrown half dead into my pickup. Benjamin's coat in the forest. And this feeling that I'm being watched every night. That makes too many things! I can't be crazy! And then there are all the stupid things I keep discovering my kids have done. And that idiot Delmas strutting around, putting his dirty hands on everything. I know it's not the same, but . . ."

I crack up completely. Reynaud takes me in his arms.

"It's all right, Sarah. It's all right."

"I don't know who's on the boat or why he's in the middle of the lake in this weather, but I don't want to leave one more question unanswered. I know none of this makes any sense, but maybe this one thing will tell us something important. About Marceau, about Jade, about all of it. The lake may have the answer."

Reynaud's face clouds over. I know nothing I'm saying holds together. But if he tells me to calm down, I'll slap him. At last, he takes one of his shotguns from the wall.

"The boat is ready to leave," he says without further ado. "Do you at least know where you're going?"

He believes me. I get my cell phone out as quickly as I can and indicate a point on the screen that has been motionless for a few minutes. Reynaud throws me a raincoat that's too big for me.

Outside, it's like the apocalypse.

We splash across the garden in the torrential rain, raising our voices to make ourselves heard. When we get to the dock at the end of the path, it's green with slippery moss. Despite everything, I manage to leap onto the boat while Reynaud unties the mooring ropes.

The wind blows across us, jolting us from side to side. We advance like crabs across the enormous swells. Reynaud pushes the thirty-horsepower outboard motor, which spits out clouds of smoke as we reach eleven knots. The bow slices through the waves, water filling the cockpit. The shore disappears in a diaphanous mist, and within a minute, we've lost our bearings and are thrown toward the shallows of Lake Geneva.

Reynaud shakes his head. "This is madness! We haven't had a storm like this in at least fifteen years!"

I stay on the alert. The lake is seething.

"Careful! Head straight into the waves, or we'll capsize."

"You must be joking. I can't see anything ahead!"

I take over the controls and hand him the phone, our one point of reference. I push the engine to its limits.

"Hey, you're going too fast!" Reynaud cries.

We've accelerated to twenty knots too quickly.

I hold on to the controls, while Reynaud braces himself at the rail as best he can. I negotiate every wave, keeping straight to our destination.

"Where is it, damn it? I can't see a thing!"

Reynaud turns, shielding his face with his hand.

"Stop, stop! What's that dot over there?"

I change tack, compensating as best I can between gusts for the swell that lifts us and the acceleration of the engine. Twice, I hear the propeller cut through the air. We lift off from the water; then the propeller shaft plunges back in and moves us forward again.

It's definitely the agency's boat.

I circle it as best I can. It looks abandoned.

Then a head emerges from the cabin, a head I recognize. Alexis.

And a second one. Rollin.

35

I see Alexis cup his hands around his mouth as if to call to us, but I don't hear him. I slow the motor as much as I can.

"We're out of fuel!" Alexis is saying.

I can't approach without the two hulls colliding. Reynaud opens one of the big chests in the cockpit and takes out a fuel can. The red paint is cracked, and it's greasy with gasoline. It's half full. He brandishes it in the air like a trophy, almost falling in the water, then screams an order to Alexis and Rollin.

"Throw us a rope, and we'll tie the can to it! It'll float and you can pull it to you!"

While Reynaud makes a bowline knot around the metal handle of the container, I notice lots of boxes floating on the surface around Alexis and Rollin's boat.

Before Reynaud has even got back on his feet, I grab the can and dive with it into the lake. I sink almost six feet, and the kingdom of silence grabs hold of me. The rope immediately goes taut, and I am pulled back to the surface. I hear muffled cries as I come back up.

"Saraaaahh!!!!"

Alexis and Rollin grab hold of me as best they can and manage to hoist me on deck. "What are you doing? Have you lost your mind?"

I'm still clinging to one of the boxes I caught hold of when I was in the water. I'm shivering with adrenaline. Reynaud, wild-eyed, is waving at me from the controls of his boat, circling us. Alexis fills the gas tank from the can, then engages the starter, and the motor shakes and throbs. As Alexis follows Reynaud in the direction of the closest dock, which is lit by a momentarily clear sky, I open the box in front of Rollin, who lowers his head.

"We'll talk about this when we get back," Alexis cries, without turning.

I look first at one, then at the other. Alexis remains focused on the complex matter of navigation. Despite the gusts, the water coming on board, the nausea, and the shivers we all have, I want to know.

"No, now! What is all this shit?"

Rollin hasn't taken his eyes off the lake. I grab him by the arm, but he breaks free.

"It's . . . it's a bit of extra income to help make ends meet. Business is tough, Sarah. The cops came and asked me a whole lot of questions. They started searching. I filled the van—I had no choice. Alexis, who knew about . . . Alexis suggested we throw everything in the lake."

Alexis hasn't missed any of this. "What are we going to tell Reynaud now, Sarah?" he asks.

I hold on to the box, hugging it a little tighter, this proof of all the lies, of everything that's been hidden from me. These were my closest friends. Friends I thought I could trust.

I feel the disappointment rising inside me. To think I've been taking risks for these people . . .

The waves are still tossing about the boat, and ahead of us, Reynaud's boat keeps disappearing under the waves and coming up again. As the shore takes shape in the distance, my thoughts collide.

"Rollin, I need to know. Have you been dealing drugs with the boat repairer's son? Tell me the truth, damn it!"

Rollin is holding his head in both hands, like a child caught in the act who finally blurts it all out and waits for his punishment.

"That little bastard discovered my . . . activities. He was going to squeal on me if I didn't supply him with dope. A stupid arrangement, but I had no choice. For the moment, at least. I planned to get him off my back eventually. I just didn't know how."

"And what about Hermione—did you think about my daughter? She hung out with the guy! Maybe Zoé too? Did you ever think he was a bad influence on our daughters?"

He bows his head. I'm stunned.

My instincts tell me that if I want to find answers about Marceau, and maybe Jade, I must stay in control. The shore is less than fifty yards away. I throw the box overboard. They both look at me.

"I'll talk to Reynaud. You two keep your mouths shut!"

~

Our shoes are drying on the rug by the front door of Reynaud's house. Reynaud has given us dry clothes, and the ones I change into in his den are too big for me. I hear voices in the living room. Reynaud is getting seriously angry.

"What the fuck were you doing on the lake? You know how dangerous it is, especially you, Rollin! You know the lake, you've been sailing! And don't try to fob me off with lies!"

I hurry in before things get nasty.

"Listen," I say to Reynaud, "now's not the time for this, not when Delmas is prying into everything. That boat isn't totally in order, to be honest. We don't need more hassle. I've caused the agency enough trouble already. I told Karen we took it to a dock not far from here."

It's a weak lie, but not entirely false. I look at Alexis and Rollin, who are also being scrutinized by Reynaud. *Come on, react!*

Alexis is the first to catch on. "We were just trying to help . . ."

"And smart as you are, neither of you thought to check the fuel gauge? Who would believe that? I ask you for the last time: What the fuck were you doing out there? If I search the boat, what will I find?"

Alexis is rattled. Reynaud won't let go—he's quite capable of turning the boat upside down. Alexis looks at me for a moment, then turns to Reynaud.

"OK, OK. In order to obtain certain contracts, I provide . . . services."

Reynaud narrows his eyes. I can't believe we have to deal with this new complication.

"What kind of services?" Reynaud asks.

Alexis grabs his backpack and empties three small dark boxes, wrapped in paper, on the table. Reynaud unwraps the contents. Gold set in Styrofoam blocks.

He looks at Alexis in astonishment. "Each one of these weighs two pounds. They must be worth about a hundred thousand dollars."

Alexis massages his forehead.

"I never do this, or almost never . . . But he's my best customer. I can't do without him financially. He sometimes asks me to cross the lake in the boat, to a rendezvous point on the Swiss side. Sometimes it's gold, sometimes diamonds, once it was a work of art. I always said a hundred thousand max. And never drugs, never coke or anything like that. The hundred thousand limit is so that it looks compatible with my assets and investments if ever I get audited. Weather like this is actually ideal—you can cross more discreetly. For today's load, it was perfect."

Again, bitterness rises in my throat. My boats are transporting drugs, gold, diamonds, and all that behind my back? I notice Alexis doesn't squeal on Rollin, whose dope has been dumped into the lake, but I can't help saying, "So, when you went out on the lake with 'customers' in order to 'sign contracts,' you were actually providing these 'services'?"

Reynaud is sharper than me. "One day you'll either end up at the bottom of the lake or in jail! Everything will depend on who gets to you first, the cops or the crooks."

"The market's been tough since the financial crisis. The only way to hold on to your customers is to be more . . . flexible. At least until the economy improves and you can diversify."

An electric shock suddenly goes through me. Is it the nervous and physical exhaustion of the last few hours, the last few days? Or a terrible premonition?

"And what about Marceau in all this? Where does that money of his come from? What will Delmas find?"

Alexis is silent.

"Marceau . . . didn't need all that," Rollin says, head bowed. "He had talent. He wasn't stupid enough to get involved in crappy schemes. I don't know where the money comes from."

A wave of emotion suddenly sweeps over us at of the mention of Marceau and the realization of his absence. Reynaud rubs his face, then opens the doors of his sideboard, takes out four glasses with one hand and a bottle of old rum with the other, and fills the glasses.

"You're going to do me the pleasure of clearing up your mess and keeping your noses clean until the investigation is over. After that, you can find another way to get by, without all this illegal shit. I have no desire to lose all the people I love before I die. I'm the one who has to go first, not you."

He raises his glass, inviting us to do the same. Our sadness wears off as we drink. I look at them in turn. We're all together. Or almost all . . . Twenty years ago, at this same table, Marceau and Jade were with us. Am I the only one to remember?

36

The storm has blown itself out, leaving behind evidence of its power everywhere.

At the agency, Benjamin is slumped on one of the couches, glued to his game console, headphones on, lost in his own world. He comes back alone from school now. He knows the route from school to the agency, especially the last part that passes the bakery. Karen has gotten him a hot chocolate, which he has finished. I stroke his hair, but he remains focused on his screen. Karen is at the computer behind the counter. I ask her if she'd like a coffee. I don't say anything when I place the cup next to her. I'm not quite sure where to begin, so I leave the initiative to her.

"Rollin brought back the boat," she says in a low voice, glancing at Benjamin. "We talked about certain things."

Hesitantly, Karen turns her cup in one direction, then the other. I know it's intolerable for her to have to admit there's a flaw in her perfect life. But today, the fault is a gaping hole. I let her continue without saying a word—it's best not to.

"Delmas came by this morning. Thanks to him, I discovered that my husband has a . . . a 'hidden talent.' I hope it won't have repercussions for the agency. It's all in Delmas's hands now. Rollin also told me about his excursion out on the lake with Alexis, up until the point where you intervened."

She's spat all this out in one go, no beating around the bush. Her face is white. I don't see any anger in it, not for the moment anyway. Rather, she seems to be in a daze.

"We'll keep this to ourselves, Karen," I say. "Delmas doesn't need to know what happened on the lake. It has nothing to do with the investigation into Marceau's death . . . or with Jade."

It's the first time I've seen Karen so vulnerable. It makes me feel less alone in my fragile state.

She turns to me.

"Delmas could put pressure on us. I can't stand the guy. He's ready to do anything, you just never know."

Karen has been carrying the agency on her shoulders since Marceau died. She needs my support, and I owe it to her.

"We'll sort this out together, Karen, as we always have."

She looks at me gratefully. We've both been suffering a series of shocks and disappointments. We both know it's not over yet. Where will the next blow come from? From wherever we least expect it. From some shadowy corner where the real evil is lurking.

~

We didn't say a word on the ride back. As soon as we got home, Benjamin grabbed his keys and rushed into the house. He hasn't taken off his cap; that's the code—I know what to expect. He'll talk to me again tonight, after dinner.

I look around at the garden. There doesn't seem to be too much damage. The storm has slightly trimmed some of the trees I should have pruned myself before spring. The dense grass, at its highest this season, looks like the day after a party. I walk to the hangar, glancing left and right. It's sturdier than it appears; nothing has moved. The Savage Bobber seems to have retreated a few yards, as if the storm scared it. The entrance could use a sweeping to get rid of the debris of plants that took shelter wherever they could.

I suddenly hear footsteps. Someone is approaching. My first reflex is to retreat into the hangar and look for a blunt instrument. Then a familiar voice calls me.

Delmas. He's like a leech these days. Considering how reluctant he was at first to start an investigation, he's certainly making up for lost time.

"Are you into repairing planes as well as boats? I thought that was your husband's territory."

I take my hands away from the toolbox. I realize I'm still wearing the clothes Reynaud lent me.

"You haven't been easy to track down today, Madame Miller," he continues. "You weren't at the agency, and you weren't at home."

"Did you have to make such a song and dance in the media?"

"I do what the higher-ups tell me to do. You know what that means, obeying instructions, not just doing as you please."

"Especially when it suits you, I guess. Do you have any news at least? What about the sling we found? What about the two boys?"

"They're in the clear. They have a cast-iron alibi for the time when your husband died. They could well have lost that sling when they were running away, and someone picked it up. We'll find an explanation. Do you still think I'm only half doing my job?"

"I'd prefer not to answer that. But are you saying you haven't made any progress?"

"I'm going to be honest with you. We didn't find anything on your husband's laptop. The hard drive was encrypted but completely empty. Just a few apps and the operating system, which we thought was strange. And then we checked it for fingerprints. Yours were there but not your husband's, and that struck us as even stranger. I don't think he wrote his novels with gloves on, do you? We cops get excited about strange things like this."

His broad-shouldered officer comes up to him. "The boy only has a tablet, the girl a laptop, a PC, like Madame Miller. No other Mac, no other backup. But I also found this . . ."

He holds out something wrapped in one of my kitchen cloths.

Delmas lifts an eyebrow. I don't have time to get a word in edgewise. I brace myself for what's to come.

"We looked carefully at all the documents you supplied us with. Like the purchase invoice for a MacBook Pro in mid-2018—I'll spare you the serial number. Unfortunately, even though these machines are very similar, the one you said was your husband's laptop isn't the one matching this invoice. That model dates from 2016. Very similar, I grant you, but not the same."

I look from one of them to the other.

"I have no idea what any of this means."

"I get the feeling anybody can come in and out of your house as they please. You'd be well advised to change the locks. In the meantime, we're going to take the rest of your computer equipment."

"Not the children's . . ."

I hear the imploring tone in my voice.

"We often know less about our nearest and dearest than we think. And a little less screen time won't hurt them."

I curse him inside. But I'm being assaulted by doubts from all directions. I thought my reserves of trust were inexhaustible—trust in life, which was so good to us, trust in my husband, my family, my friends—but that trust has been diluted with every day that's passed since Marceau died. Everything that's happening to me, everything I discover, adds to my sense of disillusionment and betrayal.

Feeling weary, just about ready to give up, I ask, "What's that in the cloth?"

"You tell us, Madame Miller."

As he opens the cloth, he tilts his head slightly and looks at me.

"As you can see, it's a gun," Delmas says, in a tone so smug it's like he's enjoying himself. "A Beretta 9mm. That's a serious weapon, Madame Miller. When were you planning to tell us about it? Because as far as I can recall, it's never been mentioned that anyone in this house has a license to carry a gun."

I can feel my hands shaking.

"I found it in Marceau's study. It was hidden in the ceiling vent."

He takes the weapon out of the cloth and examines it.

"The chamber's empty, but the weapon appears to be in good working order."

I heave a sigh and walk toward the back of the hangar. Getting up on tiptoe, I reach up to the highest shelf and take hold of a large rusty can filled with brushes that are no longer usable, the bristles hard and dry. I take them out and plunge my hand into the bottom of the can. I hand the object to Delmas, who's jubilant.

"The cartridge clip! And it's full. Sensible of you to keep it separate from the gun."

"With the children in the house, the thought of owning a gun terrifies me. When I discovered it, I put it here, away from the house. I don't know what Marceau was doing with a gun like that. And I don't want to know. Get rid of it for me."

"It's not as simple as that, Madame Miller. But with a serial number, a make, and a model, we may learn more about its *legal* owner."

His insistence on the word *legal* revives the nausea I felt earlier, just as his unbearably condescending repetitions of *Madame Miller* make me want to slap him.

The other officer makes a call on his cell phone. Without taking his eyes off me, he talks with a colleague from the squad.

"Could you check the registration of a gun we found at the Millers'? I'll text you the serial number."

Standing beside him, Delmas assumes a falsely reassuring air but can't conceal a predatory smile.

"This won't take long, Madame Miller."

Madame Miller says fuck you, you son of a bitch!

The officer announces that the gun is registered in the name of Yves Reynaud. Date of purchase: September 14, 2000.

Delmas's eyes light up.

"Well, now, things are starting to heat up, just as I like them. Our crack shot is going to receive a little social call. We don't believe in coincidences in our profession. Our friend Reynaud knows that as well as we do. He was the officer in charge of the Jade Miller case in 2001. He let her slip through his fingers, never found any trace of her. Strange, that . . . But we're not going to let *him* slip through our fingers."

37

THE MANUSCRIPT

Life is nothing but a series of small and large accidents. Apart from that, everything rests on the choices we make when faced with the blows of fate. In the case of my father's accident, we chose to hide. In the case of the car accident by the lakeshore, again we chose to hide. In the case of Jade, I *chose to hide. But you can't hide the truth with impunity, and you can't hide it forever. And it doesn't lessen the suffering. It's just a last resort that stays with us until we die—or maybe even causes our death.*

In all my books, there's a clue that could reveal the truth. I've made it a rule. And the more copies of my novels on the shelves, the greater the risk that someone would find these clues, the more tolerable my state of mind. In other words, I haven't waited for this text, which I'm rewriting constantly, to share the things I know. I am just more explicit and more comprehensive about them in this manuscript.

Every time one of my novels comes out, I have a ritual. I dive down to the wreck of my father's Savage Bobber, which is where everything began. Then I go to the place where Jade rests, the place nobody yet knows about, filled with the weight of the suffering I caused her. My father met his death in the lake; Jade left us in the forest. And by the time you read this, I will certainly have left you in the heart of the mountains. Three landscapes, three lives, three stories connected by secrets.

To silence the truth is the slowest, most toxic poison to the soul in existence. Especially when silence and lies accumulate. They don't hide behind each other. They face each other like a hall of mirrors, multiplying their destructive reflections ad infinitum.

That poison got the better of Jade. The same poison got the better of me.

38

Benjamin has withdrawn into a silence that's unusual even for him. Despite all my attempts, he hasn't opened his mouth all evening. He's cutting himself off from me, I sense. He refuses to accept the situation; he's in denial.

His resistance to Delmas, who had to intervene physically to take his tablet away as long as the investigation lasts, almost reassured me. He's defending himself, which means that at least he's reacting. But this gesture of rebellion toward an authority figure isn't like him. Even Hermione is getting worried. Right now, they're in their rooms. I don't know how to handle their distress.

I need air, and I need answers. I need all this to end before my dark thoughts get the better of me.

Outside, the sun has just disappeared behind the mountains. The lake is getting darker, the horizon fading. I walk into the garden and stop right in the middle of it. I look at the Norwegian shed in the corner of the garden, the one that Marceau and I stained for the third time last summer. How long has it been since Benjamin or Hermione has used it as a playhouse or a hiding place? The last people in there were the police. Before that, Marceau was in there about a week before his death.

My heart in my mouth, I walk to the shed, opening the squeaky door. To the left is the deep wooden tray just as I last saw it, overflowing with Marceau's and my diving equipment. To my right, shelves full of useless knickknacks, gardening equipment, rudimentary tools. Facing me, beneath the window with a view of the lake, a little desk. Marceau sometimes worked here. The floor creaks slightly beneath my feet. I remember a time when Marceau and I made love in here while the children were in the house, watching TV. I worried they might barge in suddenly, but Marceau was right: Their voices calling to each other always preceded them when they came running into the garden. Kneeling by the tray, I take out Marceau's diving suit and hug it to me. It smells of the lake. Then I take out his regulator, lift it to my mouth, open the tank, and breathe in. The darkness gradually overwhelms me. I get Marceau's watertight flashlight out of the binding of the suit. I try to turn it on, but it doesn't light. I shake it, to no avail. I remember seeing some packs of batteries in the desk drawer. I unscrew the flashlight and shake it again to extract the batteries, but nothing comes out. I look inside: A rolled-up piece of paper has been stuffed in there. I take it out—the paper is familiar, but I don't quite recognize it. I unroll it. In the fading daylight, I read these few handwritten lines:

> *I know you said, "No words." You have to admit that coming from a writer, that's paradoxical. I'm attached to the moments we've shared. Not only when you dive, but also when I smell your skin, when I feel it against mine.*
>
> *K.*

It's like a dagger thrust deep into my guts and turning slowly, making me bleed, hurting me. I sit down. I can't make sense of it. Karen and Marceau. *My* Marceau. I probe my memory, looking for details I must have missed—smiles, looks, words. I take the diving knife out of the tray and remove it from its sheath. One side is a sharp blade, the other equally sharp teeth. The thin point shines in what's left of the light. I slip it into the hollow of my hand and press as hard as I need to. The pain explodes in me. This isn't a nightmare. This time, it's worse.

~

In the garden, totally shrouded in darkness by now, I go around in circles, my fist clenched to stem the blood still gushing from my palm. I still have the handle of the knife in my other hand. In an uncontrollable impulse, I scream at the top of my lungs. The light in Benjamin's room comes on. His silhouette appears at the window. I hope he doesn't see the blade in my hand. What else will he have to face? My poor children. My life is going to pieces—even the memories are ruined. The past, the present . . . and what about tomorrow?

39

I haven't slept a wink all night, cursing as the hours pass. My anger lies deep in my belly, like a wild beast inside me ready to leap. Betrayal and lies leave the taste of sour fruit. I've kept the knife within reach, wanting to take it with me into the nightmare, if I ever fall asleep, and confront the vision of Marceau in his fall. What remains of my sanity whispers to me that weapons, anger, and exhaustion are not a good combination. But what else can I do except fight? Or die?

In the bathroom, I wrap a new bandage around my throbbing hand. I can feel the rhythm of my pain in my heartbeat. Bruises, scratches, bumps, cuts . . . there isn't a part of me that hasn't been hurt. My face is getting more and more gaunt. It feels like I'm becoming another person, that I'm moving in parallel to my own life, and other people's. That I'm sinking into the shadows, opening only the wrong doors, which lead to tragedies that destroy everything that's good in life. The only way I'll get through this is by *knowing*, with Marceau's reasons at last in front of my eyes. His damned manuscript.

~

Benjamin and Hermione left for school earlier. I walked around the house and garden for an hour. Now I'm on the shore, looking at the lake. I thought I could face Karen without letting anything show, go to the agency as if it's an ordinary morning, a morning from before the chaos started, but there's no way. All the same, I must somehow find the manuscript, without blowing everything up prematurely and risking never getting any answers.

What's in store will give me an excuse not to be in my "normal state," if I still know what that is. Delmas asked me to join him at four this afternoon to reconstruct everything we know, making it clear that the prosecutor will be there. Does he think I'm so unpredictable that he needs someone else with him? It's true—he hasn't seen the last of my outbursts.

I sit on the grass and open the radio app on my phone. I scroll through the stations and tune in to the news. With the discovery of the gun, the case is definitely heating up. Delmas hasn't held anything back—his job's on the line. The newscaster is having a field day.

"According to our sources, Captain Robin Delmas, who's leading the Miller investigation, has a suspect in custody. Do we have the culprit? It was in the early hours of the morning that Delmas's team, heavily armed, entered the home of retired police officer Yves Reynaud, a hunter who is said to have a veritable armory in his house. It was the discovery of a high-caliber handgun hidden in the house of the writer Marceau Miller that provided Delmas with this lead. The weapon in question, a Beretta 9mm, is said to have belonged to the suspect since 2000. In other words, a year before the disappearance of Jade Miller, the writer's sister, who has not been seen since August 14, 2001. The suspect claims that Marceau Miller stole it from him. But Yves Reynaud was in charge of the investigation into the Jade Miller disappearance. Could this be the missing link between the two Miller cases? The police searched the suspect's residence and discovered what amounted to a shrine dedicated to the Jade Miller case in a bunker situated beneath his house. The collection of evidence and material is the result of a twenty-year clandestine investigation that can only be called an obsession. Everything

suggests that crucial clues will emerge from this discovery. Already, never-before-seen photographs indicating an intimate relationship between Yves Reynaud and Jade Miller, who was thirty years his junior, have been uncovered. At the time he was not only a police officer, he was also an instructor of mountain guides, including Jade. Has Yves Reynaud been concealing information about the writer's sister? What really happened to her? Maybe the latest developments will bring answers. As for Marceau Miller's role in all of this, there are too many new questions to know."

PART FIVE:

THE TIME OF THE WOLVES

40

I have pins and needles in my legs. Cold has seeped into my bones, even though the temperature is mild and I'm dressed warmly. Four p.m. Everyone has taken their place at the exact spot where Marceau met his death. The prosecutor approaches Delmas, and two police officers escort Reynaud, in handcuffs, toward the crime scene. I no longer know who I see when I look at him. My old friend? The substitute father, mine and Marceau's? The man locked in his bunker with his secret obsessions who made me fear for my life? The protector of my children? I no longer know.

Alexis is next to me, Rollin a little to one side with Karen. On the ground in front of us, the outline of Marceau's body. Numbered yellow cones mark the discoveries made so far. Delmas checks the accuracy of the positions from photographs taken at the scene. Two professional mountaineers are present, fully equipped: harnesses, ice axes, ropes, magnesium bags, quickdraws, belay devices.

The prosecutor clears her throat. "Gentlemen, please proceed. The hour of death was about now, and the weather conditions are similar. That is correct, isn't it, Captain Delmas?"

Delmas nods.

"Please confirm this out loud."

"Yes, the medical examiner estimates the time of death at about four p.m., and the weather conditions were indeed similar."

One of the mountaineers begins climbing the rock face. He keeps in touch with his partner through his walkie-talkie, while securing the way with ropes and quickdraws, all the things Marceau didn't do. Madmen, extreme climbers, all of his free-solo heroes are dead: Brad Gobright, Austin Howell . . . Alex Honnold is still alive, but for how much longer? And now Marceau, dead.

I remember Marceau in the mountains, his movements so supple and precise. My hands tense and my breathing speeds up. I keep seeing Marceau's face looking at me as he falls unavoidably in my nightmares. A police officer appears at the summit, silhouetted against the sun, and my blood freezes. The mountaineer stops his climb at 230 feet, at the point where it seems most likely that Marceau came away from the rock face. He's about a hundred feet from the summit. He fixes a belay device to use as a point of reference. There was a time when Marceau taught me about all this, before he stopped using equipment.

After another fifty minutes, the mountaineer reaches the summit. He communicates with his partner on the ground.

"All stable."

The prosecutor gestures with one hand.

"OK, let's do it."

Two police officers take a dummy from the trunk of their car. It has a lead belt around its waist as ballast. Marceau weighed 150 pounds. I suddenly recall his embrace, the strength of his arms, and my heart contracts. The police officers carry the dummy to the mountaineer who has remained at the bottom. He attaches it to one of the ropes that goes up as far as his partner on the summit, then turns to the prosecutor. One look is enough.

"Hoist it up!"

The man again informs his partner through his walkie-talkie. The dummy begins its ascent, alternately gliding and hitting the rock. Once it gets to 230 feet, it stops.

"Now, everyone, please move behind the cones, sixty yards from the point of impact."

The mountaineer on the summit holds the dummy in position at the end of his rope. The police officer next to him lifts a stone weighing some six or seven pounds above his head, aiming as best he can at the dummy. At the moment of impact, the mountaineer lets go of the rope, and the dummy falls—just like in my nightmare. I feel dizzy, and Alexis grabs hold of my arm to stop me from swaying. I see Rollin lower his head and Karen hold her hands in front of her face. The dummy plummets the 230 feet in a fraction of a second. The noise as it crashes to the ground sends a shock through the gathering. There are muffled cries, jumps, then silence—the silence of sudden death. The plastic head detaches itself from the body and rolls about thirty feet. Delmas picks it up, without taking his eyes off Reynaud.

"That's how it happened, Reynaud, isn't it?" he hisses.

"You're crazy, Delmas, and you're getting it all wrong!"

The prosecutor intervenes. "That's enough. What I want right now is certainty as to the circumstances of the death. We need enough evidence to place charges."

Is the murderer here among us? Or is he elsewhere, hidden in the surrounding forest? The prosecutor and Delmas are talking with an expert and the mountaineer who's at ground level.

Karen makes a move toward me, and I turn my back on her. Not for the reasons she imagines. All in good time. Right now, everything's too confusing, too painful.

Does Alexis remain my last support? I thought seeing this reenactment would help, but it hasn't. It's merely feeding the monster in my head. Why is that monster torturing me like this?

41

Delmas's men pack up the hardware, and everyone goes back down to the parking lot. The prosecutor is the first to leave. The mountaineers are dismissed. I exchange glances with Reynaud, who's sitting in the back seat of the police car, still in custody. I'm much more used to seeing him at the wheel of the police car with criminals in the back, but now everything is turned around.

Karen tries to approach me again, and this time when I turn away, she knows it. Rollin grabs her by the arm and walks her to their car. She's keeping the children this evening. They will spend the night there with Zoé. It was Alexis who suggested it, thinking that the day's events would be grueling for me. He probably didn't realize quite how grueling.

He places his arm around my shoulder. I don't have the strength to push it away or lean into it.

"What can I do to cheer you up?"

It's like my brain is paralyzed, incapable of handling anything.

"I really don't know . . . Leave me alone, I think."

"That may not be the best thing, Sarah."

I take a deep breath. "It's what I need. I just want to be alone."

Alexis shakes his head and goes back to his car. I stand there and watch as all the cars, one after another, leave.

Everything is quiet again, and I am alone in the calm of nature.

Exhausted, I get into my pickup and tilt the seat back slightly. I keep the door open, allowing the late-afternoon breeze from the Alpine pastures to caress my face like a tender hand. I close my eyes, letting my senses open to the natural world around me. The resin of the spruce trees mingles with the scent of the blue gentian on the slopes and balsam from the centuries-old larches. The last rays of the sun warm the limestone, liberating the mineral scent so characteristic of these mountains. An Alpine chough lets out its distinctive cry, short and repetitive, almost metallic, which echoes against the walls of rock and fades into the distance, swallowed by the forest. The rustling of the high Alpine grasses reminds me how it felt to hide in the meadows as a child.

I wait for my energy to return, but exhaustion gets the best of me. Sleepless nights have sucked my last ounce of vitality. Sleep takes hold of me like a dark hand I don't see coming.

I open my eyes. According to the dashboard clock, it's 6:20 p.m. I've slept like a log for more than an hour. I get out in a daze, the nightmare hovering everywhere around me. I'm in it, and it's in me. I want to challenge it, ward it off. It isn't here, at the foot of the rock face that took Marceau from me, that things will be decided. I stare up resolutely at the summit. I start up the path, which is soon overrun with tall grass. I try to walk where it's been flattened by the comings and goings of the police. A bird of prey circles about 150 feet above my head. The wind has dropped, marking the end of the day.

The minutes pass slowly. I haven't brought anything to drink, I'm not wearing the right kind of shoes—I'm not respecting any of the rules. I ignore all the warning lights that are flashing. I don't give a damn. After climbing with difficulty for about a quarter of a mile, I enter the forest.

The last stage before the heights. From here on, it's impossible to detect the slightest trace of anyone having passed through this untamed world. I hold on to the tree trunks to help me climb. The sky filters through the foliage in the distance. The closer I get, the less air there seems to be. At last, I reach the natural platform I reached with Reynaud, what seems like an eternity ago.

The place is still as bare, the panoramic view as dizzying. I take one step, then another, closer and closer to the void. I sway and look down at the ground seven hundred feet below. I see again the heavy stone falling, the dummy abruptly pulling away from the rock face, like Marceau losing his footing. I keep advancing, only about a foot from the edge. I make out the trace of the dummy hitting the ground. Then everything starts to whirl around me, and I fall to my knees. Just like in my nightmare, I stretch out my arms to the void, but they're too short to hold Marceau back from his fall . . . I lie down on the ground. If I wanted to, I could end it all right now. I could let myself topple over the edge, arms first.

Then I snap out of it.

I slowly move back, retreating from the edge of the cliff. Once I'm back on my feet, I walk as fast as I can toward the forest.

A shot rings out among the trees. The bark of a tree explodes close to me.

I dive onto the ground, and my survival instincts kick in. I start running, jumping over branches, zigzagging between trees. I fix on the largest tree some fifteen yards away and, not detecting any movement in my field of vision, run toward it. A second shot. I dive again. I listen hard. I need to isolate the source, estimate the distance. I stay in a ball at the foot of the trunk and weigh what to do next. Still no movement. It's impossible to figure out where the shots are coming from.

I burst out of my hiding place, and a third shot hits a nearby tree. I stifle a scream and continue running. I'm expecting another shot, but nothing comes. I weave between the trees, hoping to make myself harder to track, and I go even farther into the forest. My leg muscles are starting to cramp, but I ignore the pain. Another shot, farther away this time. I run at high speed back down the way I climbed. As I run, I keep in mind that, if need be, I could lie in the tall grass and still be able to advance unseen—but that would be too slow. Maybe Marceau was right to own a gun. The pickup is now only about thirty yards away. I'm there! I throw myself at the door and fumble to fit the key in the lock.

As I do so, I notice that the front tire is flat. I crouch down and circle the car, looking around. No noise, no movement . . . and none of the other tires are flat. I move away, hide, and watch. Still no suspicious noise, even though it's impossible to take a step without cracking a branch. The minutes pass. I'm thirsty and I'm tired. I have to move.

I go back to the car and examine the burst tire. There's a definite cut on the side, as if it's been slashed with a knife. Somebody doesn't want me here. Still silence, no movement around me. I unhook the spare tire, take out the jack, and start changing the tire as quickly as I can. The nuts don't resist me for very long. The awareness that every second counts galvanizes me. I turn the crank handle a dozen times. The pickup's shock absorbers creak as the vehicle rises the few inches necessary to remove the wheel. With each movement, I twist my neck to probe the surroundings. Nobody, no sign of the shooter. I switch the tires, quickly fix half the nuts—the others I can do later. I release the pressure of the jack, throw it aside, climb in, and set off at top speed, head down.

42

My legs and hands are shaking as I try to catch my breath. The sun is sinking behind the mountains, casting disturbing shadows on the road. Every bend takes me closer to the house, but the thought that someone might be following me keeps me moving fast. This region I love so much is starting to seem like hostile territory. I keep to this excessive speed all the way home. I park the pickup outside the hangar, facing forward, ready to leave again in a hurry. No downtime, no respite for me. Dusk is falling; the house is gradually fading into the darkness. Can I finally breathe freely, can I feel safe, at least temporarily? The moon is reflected on a smooth surface near the house. Could it be . . . the hood of Alexis's Porsche? But there is no light in the house, nobody in the garden, it seems. I advance cautiously toward the lake and gradually make out a figure sitting on the landing stage, legs dangling over the water. Alexis waves at me as I advance toward him.

"I just wanted to make sure you'd got back. This has been a terrible day for all of us."

Next to him, a bottle of brandy, a third empty. He reaches it out to me so that I can drink straight from the bottle, like he's doing, the way we drank when we were twenty, when Jade and Marceau were still alive. I sit down, breathing hard, legs still shaking. The lake is calm, the reflections of the stars sharper as the sky turns black.

"Even a few weeks ago, I would never have imagined anything worse."

I grab the bottle and take a swig, then another. It's strong and gentle at the same time, a deceptive nectar if you don't take care. Complex aromas of vanilla, honey, spices. The label says, *Cognac Baron Otard XO*.

"Nobody would have imagined it, Sarah. Now we have to learn to cope."

"I was almost killed just now."

He looks at me, concerned. "What do you mean?"

"Someone shot at me in the forest. On the Dent du Vélan."

I take a third swig.

"After the reenactment? We have to tell Delmas. Did you see anything?"

"No, as usual. I have no actual evidence. Do you think I'm just crazy?"

"No, it means Delmas has to get moving, and that you need to be careful. Maybe you ran into . . . I don't know . . . poachers?"

"How do you know there are poachers there?"

"Because there are poachers everywhere around here."

"Yes, even out on the lake, poaching gold."

He smiles awkwardly. "I'm really sorry, Sarah. I was stupid."

Silence falls between us. My thoughts wander, and the adrenaline running through my body is decreasing, numbed by the brandy now coursing through my veins.

"Marceau had already started to withdraw before Jade disappeared. But afterward, he got even worse. His eccentricities took over, even if I didn't want to see it. I got used to his absences. I didn't want to pry. I just wanted to enjoy him when we were together."

"We all got used to it. That was Marceau."

I turn to Alexis, who's looking at his reflection in the water. "Look at me, Alexis."

He lifts his head.

"Did Marceau ever share . . . anything particular with you? A thing I ought to have known, or not. You were very close. You must tell me. Did he know about your 'services' on the lake? You must have had secrets you shared."

Alexis's legs move gently above the surface of the lake. "With Marceau, it was always a one-way street. I realize now it was the same for you, Sarah. I'm sorry. We've all done stupid things from time to time. But whatever Marceau did, he kept it secret."

The palpitations I've been feeling all day are getting stronger, but I pretend I'm feeling calm.

"So he never told you what he was doing with Karen, for example?"

"Karen? What are you talking about?"

He looks as helpless as I must have looked when I discovered the note in the flashlight.

I gather my courage.

"He was having an affair with her. I want you to keep this strictly to yourself, for now at least. I want to be able to talk to Karen first, when I'm ready."

He's speechless.

"Pass me the bottle, Alexis, let's finish it."

I drink what's left of the brandy, and Alexis gently helps me to my feet as he tries to process the shock. I take his face in my hands and press my lips to his lips. I don't want to be afraid, at least for one night.

"Stay with me tonight, Alexis."

He doesn't let go of my hand until we get to the house. I lock the door behind us. In the darkness, I lead him to my bedroom. We throw our clothes on the floor, and he runs his hands over my neck, my breasts, caresses them, licks them, and then he moves his hand farther down. I take hold of his face and kiss him again as we make love. A dam breaks inside me as heat rises from the pit of my stomach. Our bodies mingle together. Our lovemaking protects me and takes me to another place. Then I arch with desire, and pleasure floods over us.

43

KAREN

The children are asleep at last. The video games are not great, but it's the only way I've found to focus their attention on something other than the drama that's going on. They're going to have to learn how to cope with what's happened, to manage it. Like all of us, like me.

I wrap a scarf around my shoulders and go out to find Rollin in his damn garage. The door is wide open, and he is sanding a piece of chestnut, fine dust hovering around him. I doubt if he even knows the purpose of what he's doing. It looks like he's working away at this piece as if he wants to sand it down to nothing. He's seen me, and he doesn't stop. I stand there watching him, not saying a word. I grab his forearm with one hand and obstruct his sanding block with the other.

"Stop!"

He frees his forearm from my hand and lowers his eyes.

"I've been an idiot, I know," he says. "Delmas wants to see me again. He's grilling me slowly. I have to give him names, but he gets angry when they don't lead anywhere. He says all the information I give him is bullshit. One of his team is sticking to me like glue now. I'm trapped."

"Thanks to all the stupid things you've done, we're both fucked. But that's not the worst of it. There's something else that Delmas is going to find out, so listen to me, Rollin, and look me straight in the eyes! You're going to do exactly what I tell you, OK? And don't start moaning."

"What . . . what's he going to find out?"

I take a deep breath and let him have it. "He's going to find out that Marceau and I were having an affair, and that's going to make you a suspect. I don't know what Sarah's plotting, but I sense it's not going to be good. She *knows* stuff."

Rollin sits down on his stool, stunned. "You and Marceau? Karen . . ."

It's a shock for him to see the true face of his little Karen. She's no longer his perfect wife, understanding at all times, always there to cover for the stupid things he does. But now's not the time for self-pity or revenge. The stakes are too real.

"It's a good thing the cops are investigating you, Rollin, but you don't have a good alibi for the day Marceau died. They won't find much, apart from one solid piece of evidence from the day of Marceau's death, which I am going to arrange. Because you didn't do anything, right? It wasn't you. We have a daughter, we need to think about her future, we're not going to torpedo everything now."

"I don't understand."

"In repairing one of your messes, I'm going to clean up another. Delmas told me just enough for my plan to work. I just need a little dope. And thanks to your negligence, I have some. You were always leaving it all over the place so that I've managed to put together a nice little stash . . . enough for what I have in mind, anyway. All the same, I need a piece of information. The baker's apprentice you were supposed to deliver to in Saint-Gingolph can't be happy to have lost his dope, can he? How much was he expecting? And don't tell me you don't remember."

Rollin is thinking, which is a good sign. I see it in his eyes. He's so predictable.

"It was three hundred grams . . . actually, more like two hundred, I think."

Hopeless. He can't even remember that.

"Then it's going to be his lucky day. For five hundred grams, he'll confirm that you regularly came in the middle of the afternoon, especially the day Marceau died. That way, he gets his three hundred or two hundred grams, with an actual bonus. You have to go there about four o'clock tomorrow afternoon. I'll have done what I need to do first. When he sees you, he'll act like everything's normal. Just let yourself be followed by the cops, give them a bit of a runaround. Do you think you could do that?"

"The cops?"

"The cops will pounce on you, Rollin! They'll catch you in the act. The two of you will be questioned about drug trafficking, which will keep them quite busy. Except that this time the guy will give you nothing but bread, prepared in advance, with your name on it, 'like he does every week'—you know, bread for your sandwiches. I think it's a brilliant idea. And you'll tell the police you love their bread, and that they give you a special price. The cops will understand why. You'll have to talk a bit about the drug trafficking, obviously. But whatever happens, it'll be established that you were there the day Marceau died. You can't commit two crimes at the same time, can you? Unless you're a genius."

44

I'm on the edge of the void, barely able to breathe. I hold out my arms, and . . . this time it isn't Marceau falling into the void, but Karen. Her face goes through all the states I'm familiar with in her—tenderness, contempt, anger, astonishment—loose hair floating in the air, before she crashes to the ground. I emerge from my nightmare, soaked to the skin, my chest heaving. It's 3:05 a.m. Alexis is still asleep beside me.

I leave the room and go into Marceau's study. The police have taken everything from his writing desk, except for the framed photograph of him at the controls of his plane, face turned while the plane heads straight for the snowcapped mountains. I take the photograph in my hands. He's smiling. I run my finger over his face. In the reflection of his aviator glasses, I can see Alexis, his head in a helmet, taking the photo.

But for the first time, I notice something else. I take the magnifying glass from the desk drawer filled with Marceau's odds and ends. The detail I missed is a lock of blonde hair peeking out of the passenger's helmet. Karen's hair. The same Karen who always said she was incapable of flying in a small plane like that.

And I remember Alexis, proud as a peacock, claiming to have taken this photograph. The bastard lied to me. He knew. Still stunned, I feel the need to get a breath of fresh air. I go down the stairs and run barefoot to the hangar. I undo the fastening of the Savage Bobber's engine hood and tear out all the cables I can get hold of. When I can't do any more damage with my hands, I open the toolbox and go at it with a hammer.

I hammer to destroy, I hammer to hurt, I hammer for the truth, and to free myself.

My hand is killing me, but I keep hammering. The engine is pissing fuel, I hammer. Karen is a slut, I hammer. Marceau is dead, I hammer. Alexis and Rollin are bastards, I hammer. I continue without stopping until I am completely exhausted. I hammer out my anger mixed with tears.

I gradually emerge from this fit of madness, my hand throbbing. I've destroyed everything I could get my hands on. The guts of Marceau's plane are everywhere, as if I've performed some crazy surgical operation.

I've even wrecked the metal plate bearing the make, model, and serial number of the plane. There's nothing more to break. This ill-omened series of numbers is still just about readable, and like a code that unlocks a well-guarded access point, my intuition comes back and whispers in my ear.

I feel a violent rush of adrenaline.

Shit, these numbers . . .

45

THE MANUSCRIPT

Jade and I were almost like twins. Born the same year, sometimes sharing the same homeroom class, both conscious of having to grow up fast after Dad's accident. All these things linked us, in life as in death, as if attached to one another by invisible handcuffs. Jade couldn't fall, or she would take me with her. Anytime she fell, I helped her get up. But there was one time, and only one, when I listened to my heart, and that was about Sarah. I wasn't paying attention—not because I was moving away from my sister, but in order to look toward another future, a future without all the things left unsaid, the lies.

Jade chose that moment to leave us. I was so angry at her. I was so angry at myself. In my way, I had to break the chain that bound us. But I hadn't broken the bracelet that continues to hurt my wrist.

After the investigation, I had to learn how to live with her ghost. While the soul may escape, secrets endure. They make it hard for those left behind to rest. It's now my turn to divest myself of the burden. I would, however, like to give those who survive me a chance to break the curse of the Millers.

And what else but the truth can set us free?

46

I stink of gasoline, anger, and love, but I get the feeling I am finally on to something.

Still barefoot, I run to the house, noiselessly put my shoes on, and in the darkness look for Alexis's jacket and take his car keys from the pocket. His Porsche is a lot faster than my pickup, which often threatens to give up the ghost. I close the door gently, then hurry to the bottom of the garden to get my diving gear from the shed. Suit, flippers, mask, flashlight, regulator, bottle, knife, line, life preserver, stabilizing vest, weights—and all the gear fits snugly beneath the hood of the Porsche. I set off for the office, making good use of Alexis's car. At this hour of the morning—it's not even four a.m.—the road is deserted. I speed along, intoxicated by the thought that Marceau's silences and mysteries will finally be revealed to me.

~

I leave the Porsche in the first parking space outside the office and go straight to the key closet, where I take the key to our most powerful boat. Not even bothering to shut the door behind me, I get the diving gear out of the car and carry it to the dock, throwing it into the cockpit of the boat. I leap onto the deck and undo the first mooring rope, start the motor, free the rear mooring line, and push the lever straight to half speed. The boat lifts, its nose toward the still-starry sky, creating waves that make the other boats around it dance. An immaculate, effervescent wake emerges on the surface of the still black water like the tail of a shooting star. I push the lever to three-quarters. The bow of the boat is now suspended above the lake. I draw a curve in the water, orienting myself toward the spot where Marceau's father's plane went down thirty years ago.

The jumble of figures at the end of the file name in the printer's history, the ones Delmas was trying to work out the meaning of, wasn't a date or number given to that version of *The Story of Marceau Miller*. It was the serial number of the plane at the bottom of the lake! It wasn't until I smashed up the engine of Marceau's plane, a replica from the same period as his father's, that I realized it.

What an ironic twist of fate!

The lights on the shore help me know which direction to head. I know my lake, and I pinpoint the location with the help of the GPS. I cast out the anchor, which sinks straight down; the chain unrolls fast and touches bottom at exactly ninety feet. The wreck must be within a radius of about thirty feet around me. I put on my gear by the light of the moon. My tank is half full—it'll be enough.

I'm used to diving, though I don't usually go so deep. I use my gear most often for inspecting the hulls of our boats or for helping our customers when they get the boat caught in ropes or nets. The boat I've borrowed isn't a dive boat, but I manage to hurl myself into the water without any problem.

The beam of my flashlight illuminates the plankton hanging in the water. I submerge, kicking hard with my flippers, and I go straight down, headfirst, as quickly as possible. Thirty feet, sixty feet . . . My time is limited, the pressure is crushing, and it helps me gain speed. The air I breathe is more and more compressed, and my heartbeat slows. I focus on keeping my mind clear and compensating for the first effects on my brain.

At last, the beam of light illuminates the bottom of the lake, both chasing away and attracting fish disturbed by my intrusion. I keep a distance of four feet or so from the bed to avoid kicking up swirls of debris that would reduce my visibility. The bottom is lunar in places, devoid of all flora. I circle like a shark around its prey.

Suddenly the tail of the plane looms out of the darkness. I beat my flippers vigorously, expelling a large volume of air from my regulator, a cloud of bubbles surrounding me. I grab hold of the tubular structure of the plane. It's strangely free of seaweed, at least on the upper parts and the cockpit. Is that Marceau's doing? I aim my flashlight inside, then on the outside. The plane is lying on the bed, slightly sunken in. I check the gauge of my tank, and there's only a third left. I've used much more oxygen than I expected. I swim faster in search of traces likely to indicate which parts of the plane have been most "explored." I put the flashlight down on the bed, angled toward the plane—my only beacon in this world of total darkness. With both hands now free, I can explore the inside of the wreck, but I've stirred up silt and can no longer make anything out, or hardly anything. I don't have time to wait for the cloud to disperse. My breathing is too rapid. I recover the flashlight and shine it on the passenger seat in the back of the plane. I try to move the seat forward but can't. I slip my hand under it. I feel something rectangular. I can only get hold of it by raising or shifting the seat. I push down on the bed and manage to move the seat, with a metal clang that spreads like a wave all around me. I pull on the object, and it begins to come out, then gets jammed. With the flashlight as a hammer, I bang on it. It advances a little more with every blow. I've almost got it when the flashlight goes out and does not turn back on. Total darkness.

I pull on the object again, and at last it's out, and I hug it to me. The biting cold at the bottom of the lake is seeping through my suit, which is too thin. I try to remember the structure of the plane in order to grope my way out of it. I hit myself on one side, and my gear snags on the other. I'm way past the time for a quick dive. In this opaque blackness, I'm going to have to make sure of a pause for decompression of five minutes at least fifteen feet below the surface to avoid a problem. I swim toward the surface, guided by the decreasing pressure in my ears and my body. I can't see anything, so there's no way to read my equipment to know how deep I am or how much air I have left. In my head, I start to count the seconds, then the minutes. After three, nothing more comes when I pull on my regulator. The tank is empty. My flippers beat against the darkness while my head gets ready to break the surface.

At last, I can breathe again.

Without wasting a moment, I look around for the boat. I spot it about forty yards away, lit by the halo of the moon. I start swimming as best I can while still holding tight to my precious find. There's no way I'm going to let it sink.

The surface of the lake is still tonight. I grab hold of the bow of the boat, hoist myself up with one arm, and drop the package and the rest of my gear into the cockpit. The tank knocks loudly against the deck of the boat. Then, with what strength I have left in my arms, I somehow manage to climb back onto the boat, supporting my knee on a bracket.

As soon as I'm sitting, I inspect what I've brought up from the depths. It's in a hermetically sealed bag made from a thick synthetic material, compressed by the pressure of the water. Using my knife, I gently pierce one of the sides and move the edges apart.

The manuscript.

At last.

On the first page, the words *The Story of Marceau Miller.*

PART SIX:

OUT OF THE MISTS

47

Dawn is breaking. Still sitting on the boat in the middle of the lake, I prepare to discover Marceau's secrets, to understand the man I lived with for so long.

Who were you really, Marceau Miller?

Although this manuscript has been absorbing my thoughts for days, to the point where I sometimes thought it might drive me crazy, I hesitate now to start reading it. I look at its first words without daring to decipher them immediately. I know the way he writes, I know the way he says things. But this time, nothing is invented. I recognize everything: the places, the events, the characters. They have names: Jade, Alexis, Rollin, Reynaud, Hermione, Benjamin, Zoé, Louise, Marceau, Sarah.

The bundles of banknotes in the duffel bag correspond to the exact amount of the royalties I earned for my first novel, $3,175,000. Money I couldn't use. The success of the book had its roots in accidents, secrets, and tragedies. Without all that suffering, I would never have taken refuge in writing, would never have invented other lives to escape the real world, at least a little. I could never *have imagined that these dark experiences would give my novels a soul, light when all I saw was darkness.*

I was the puppet of my own story. The curtains opened, leaving me alone to face the public that adored me. I tried my best to stop writing. It wasn't pressure from my publisher or the expectations of my readers or the obligation to make a living that made me go back to work after that first novel. You can't stop cooling a nuclear reactor, or it explodes. Even if the way you have found to escape that fate exposes you to radiation, you continue. When the towers of the World Trade Center were an inferno, nothing could stop their occupants from jumping, not even the certainty that they would die.

This money belongs to all those who bore these tragedies. The tragedy of my father, the tragedy of the car accident by the shore of the lake, the tragedy of Jade.

I think of all those passages I found so authentic, and sometimes so troubling, in his novels. Now I realize why. I'll have to read them again in a different way. Understanding Marceau, here, like this, is shaking me to the core.

Day is breaking over the lake; the first rays of the sun are warming my back, encouraging me to continue reading. I'm scared to think what else I might discover. Jade was my true friend. She told me everything. She had sworn she would tell me everything.

A new chapter starts with a page bearing the title: "How it all started: Jade's secret."

We were ten and nine, respectively—children. Our relationship was symbiotic, magnetic. It didn't seem as if anything could ever break our bond. We spent so much time playing together, especially in the big hangar, where our father kept and maintained his Savage Bobber. When he was away, we amused ourselves on that beautiful plane. I was the pilot, Jade the mechanic. We imagined we were in charge of the controls, the tools, the settings, just like adults. The plane was a giant toy, a fabulous playground. But Jade took the game and her skills as a mechanic too seriously, and she innocently touched something in the plane's precision engine. When our father took off that morning, we had no idea that we had sentenced him to death. The engine failed above the lake, no doubt at the worst possible moment, in the course of a delicate maneuver. It was our fault he died.

So, Jade and Marceau shared a terrible guilt, and I never saw or felt anything of this secret drama . . . The remains have been slumbering at the bottom of the lake for thirty years. My stomach tightens, and I'm filled with sadness and regret.

When I made darling Jade swear never to say a word, especially not to Mom, that's when things really started to go out of control.

Our mother was crushed, and she clung to us. At first, the secret was less burdensome than the actual loss of our father, but then, as time passed, guilt took over from grief. And the more years that went by, the bigger the mountain of guilt became. How could we admit to such a thing after six months, a year, five, ten years had passed? When our mother died of cancer, Jade tried to kill herself. She was convinced that our mother had been eaten away inside by her husband's death. My sister was more fragile than me, I should have known that, but the damage had been done. Our adult lives were starting; we were looking toward the future. But for Jade, a crack had opened, and her fragility was exposed, up until the fatal trigger, the year we turned twenty.

My breathing is so fast now, it's as if I'm on a tough climb. I have to continue, I have to know the whole truth.

A new chapter: "The accident by the lake."

But there's nothing after this title. The chapter has disappeared—or maybe it was never written? In its place, another page with a chapter title: “The day Jade disappeared.”

But again, there’s no corresponding chapter. A scream escapes me.

There’s one last sheet of paper. I cling to the writing on it and reread it several times. I don’t believe it—something cracks inside me. A dam erected twenty years ago, when Jade disappeared, abruptly collapses. The pain, so long held in, flows out like an uncontrollable torrent. I can’t breathe. Sobs rise from the depths of my being, primitive sobs I don’t recognize, two decades of contained grief at last exploding. When I catch my breath, I scream her name—*Jade!*—as if my broken voice could bring her back.

48

The pages are spread all around me. The surface of the lake begins to glow as the morning wind rises. I put the pages back in order and place the manuscript safely in the cabin of the boat. I slide my hand over the tattoo on my ankle—our tattoo, Jade's and mine—that captures our lake, the mountains, and . . . the plane, which she made me swear never to forget. I miss her voice, I miss her sensitivity, I miss everything about her. I've never known another friendship like it, and I've never recovered from her disappearance.

The boat is advancing slowly toward the shore now, the wind on my skin. I am aware of what might happen now, everything I'm about to unleash. It's still very early, and as I get closer to the dock, I don't see anyone. It appears to be a day like any other. But what I have to share in the next few hours will change everything. Will I have to explain it all to Louise eventually?

The manuscript under my arm, I hurry along the dock and take Marceau's last three books from the shelf in the office. I drop everything on the passenger seat of the Porsche and squeal out of the agency parking lot. The car seems to pick up on my nervousness better than a lie detector. The miles fly past as I drive toward Thonon-les-Bains. On the D25, approaching Sciez, I pass my pickup coming in the other direction. Alexis is at the wheel, and of course he immediately recognizes his Porsche. In the rearview mirror, I see him do a U-turn to follow me. I press my foot down on the accelerator. Alexis must have woken up and, not finding me, thought I must be at the agency.

~

I enter the police building and hurry to Delmas's door, opening it without knocking.

"Please make yourself at home, Madame Miller. Have you brought me a coffee?"

"No, a corpse."

Delmas looks me up and down. His gaze comes to rest on the manuscript and the books.

"Close the door behind you."

I put the manuscript on his desk.

"You should have looked at the bottom of the lake," I say. "The number following the name of the file in the printer corresponded to the serial number of the plane that crashed in the lake."

Delmas's mouth falls open.

"Go straight to the last page."

Delmas takes the last sheet of the manuscript.

Nobody could know, not you, not Reynaud. I've always acted alone. In every one of my novels, Jade appears. On the spines of the books, there are two watermarks: two sets of numbers, for latitude and longitude, one before the title and one after it, above the author's name. They correspond to the place where Jade's body has been lying since the day she died. I passed off this eccentricity as superstition to my publisher, who never had any other choice but to accept my special requests. The marks were almost invisible, and he didn't really care.

Delmas looks up at me. For the first time, I have the impression he's really looking at me.

"Well done," he says. "We turned Reynaud's place upside down, looked into every aspect of his life, and this thing you've found . . . would seem to exonerate him. It's too early to say, but it might be the old fool is just a stubborn man who wouldn't let go."

"Maybe he'll finally be able to close the case."

"Madame Miller, I don't know what will happen, but I can promise you one thing: I'll never end up like Reynaud."

49

The lake is bathed in sunlight. On the D1005, the Porsche skims along the road. I pass through Lugrin, and the expanse of water disappears from view as I enter a forested area near Meillerie. Before I left the station, Delmas called the prosecutor, and they had a brief conversation, agreeing to meet at the scene without delay. A helicopter has been mobilized.

I slow down when I get to the path that leads to Reynaud's house. It's much less manageable in a Porsche. I hear the undercarriage scrape on the central grassy strip, and I don't care. Alexis can repair his old banger himself. Released from custody, Reynaud is already outside, ready to leave.

As I get out, I can see him making a face at the Porsche. He shakes his head but doesn't have the strength to tell me what he's thinking, and I couldn't say if the light in his eyes reflects weariness, a profound sadness, or relief.

"I just heard on the radio they've located Jade's body. Is that true, Sarah?"

"Yes. And not so far from us, in the forest, in the mountains just near here."

"Damn it, Sarah, I looked everywhere! How is it possible?"

"Marceau knew the mountains and the forests much better than you. You may have taught him the rudiments, but the pupil surpassed the master. He acted alone. Nobody else could have known."

"So he was the one who hid the body. I had nothing to do with it, I swear to you, Sarah! I didn't know. And to think that for twenty years, he and I searched together. And all that time, he knew . . . What the fuck?"

I open the door of his SUV and get in the passenger seat. I've decided I'm not going to speculate anymore. I'm not going to look for an explanation for what Marceau did or wonder about Reynaud's possible complicity.

Reynaud takes the wheel. I locate the destination on the GPS. Reynaud's eyes have glazed over. He looks like he's somewhere else.

"We must have been past there at least ten times. It's like he was deliberately leading me there."

On the way, I tell him about the serial number, the manuscript, the missing chapters. His silence breaks my heart. I've never seen him cry before today. His tears, more than any rational explanation I could be given, convinces me once and for all of his innocence. After a few minutes, he bangs his fist on the steering wheel, his rage palpable. As we proceed onto the sinewy mountain roads, we recognize the throbbing noise of a helicopter flying at low altitude, probably coming in to land somewhere nearby.

The road continues, but we can't navigate it with the SUV, so we continue on foot, GPS in hand. We enter the thick forest, taking the best shortcut we can to get to the location. After a few challenging miles, Reynaud points to a marked path.

"In terms of time, it'll be quicker if we take that path, even if it does mean a bit of a detour. The forest is slowing us down—it's too dense."

The helicopter passes over our heads again and lands in a little clearing. We see a police officer and the pilot. We veer away so they do not notice us, and continue on our way.

Delmas doesn't seem surprised when we show up. The prosecutor is looking into a hole dug by two officers still holding their shovels. A medical examiner is crouching beside him, next to what looks like a collection of human remains. Delmas tells him to share what he knows.

"The bones we found belong to a young woman, probably about twenty, which may correspond to the description given at the time of your search, Reynaud."

Reynaud approaches the body. He points to some pieces of metal that haven't yet been cleaned and asks the expert to inspect them immediately. The man begins with a climbing clip covered in earth. It's broken, but the steel is still in good condition. He rubs it carefully to reveal an inscription carved in the metal.

"There's something here . . . not a serial number . . . a name: *Marceau.*"

Reynaud shakes his head, as if he's had a knockout blow.

"And with that clip, he left his signature, like in his novels."

The medical examiner continues his work. We watch, dazed, each of us lost in our own thoughts. The man finally gets to his feet and takes off his mask. He holds his cell phone next to his mouth to record his observations.

"Death was caused by a fall. Broken legs, three ribs broken on the right side. One of the arms is also broken. Shock at the top of the head, but it's certain the lower part of the body made contact with the ground first, the injury there considerable. Then the head hit the ground. Estimate of the height of the fall: about fifty feet."

"So, not suicide, as Marceau Miller implies at the end of his manuscript," Delmas says. "Jumping fifty feet wouldn't guarantee you'd kill yourself. It doesn't fit."

"Probably not."

Reynaud and I exchange desperate glances.

"There are crucial chapters missing from the manuscript," Delmas continues. "The criminal, whoever he is, wouldn't have just cut pages out; he would have got rid of the whole thing. Allowing us to find the body is a risk too great for him. As for Marceau Miller, omitting the vital parts of his story would be contrary to the mission he gave himself. Who could have taken the missing pages and left the rest of the manuscript? And why?"

Delmas and Reynaud are missing one important detail, which doesn't escape me. I am the only person at the moment to see it.

50

The remains of Jade's body are taken away for a postmortem. Delmas and the prosecutor leave in the helicopter, while Reynaud and I walk back along the forest path, moving cautiously, both of us still dazed, trying to get our heads around the new, insoluble equation.

Reynaud walks ahead of me, more silent than ever. He's digesting all the years of his failed investigation, his memories, the painful end of his career. It's a door that still resists being closed. All the same, things have changed. Reynaud holds out his hand to help me across a tree trunk lying across the path.

"When Marceau and I were in the forest the first few times, I was always in front. Then he quickly took command. He was the one who traced our routes on the map, who took the initiative. He always explained things so well and told me so many things I didn't know about Jade. I loved hearing him talk about her."

Reynaud's throat tightens. I lower my eyes. It hurts me too. As I lift my leg to cross the obstacle, my ankle is revealed. Reynaud places a hand on my shin, stopping me.

"That tattoo . . . it's the same as Jade's . . ."

"Yes, don't you remember? She asked me to get it, and we had them done on the same day. It was her drawing, her idea. Now that I think of it, it was a little like a confession . . . about her father. The plane. She didn't dare tell me, but she made me put it on my skin for the rest of my life . . ."

Reynaud gently pulls the hem of my pants down to cover my ankle, and we resume walking, the sounds of nature enveloping us. Branches crack beneath our feet. The trees surround me like old friends, their massive trunks offering a silent comfort. I slow down and put my hand on the rough bark of a centuries-old oak, letting its tranquil strength anchor me in the present. The air is laden with humus and resin, scents that remind me that life continues its immutable cycle, despite our human tragedies. A slight breeze rustles the leaves above our heads, as if whispering secrets I dread to hear. And yet, as always, the forest calms me, its thousand-year-old presence healing me as only it can.

Once we get back in the SUV and on the road, Reynaud switches on the radio. The case has burst wide open now. Reynaud's name is mentioned. Extracts of interviews from the original investigation are aired, everything that's been dormant for twenty years is now coming back to life, and the whole country is riveted. On my phone, there are dozens of texts, including many from unknown numbers—reporters, almost certainly. And one from Marceau's publisher, Édouard, blunt and to the point:

> When can we meet to discuss Marceau's unpublished manuscript? You do have it, don't you?

At other times, all this intrusion would have made me nauseous, but my mind is elsewhere. A terrible thought keeps nagging at me, and I have to verify it. I try to connect my memories. Some don't fit, while others come together like the pieces of a jigsaw puzzle with an unexpected design.

We reach Reynaud's house. He suggests I stay for a while and have something to eat or drink while I gather my thoughts, but I decline and drive off in the Porsche. I have to get back. I have to understand what happened before anybody else does. I have to be sure.

~

Outside our house, police officers are holding back a horde of reporters. It's early afternoon. Our house has become a circus attraction. At least Delmas's team is protecting it. Maybe he's not so bad when it comes down to it. I drive through the crowd, regretting that I'm being photographed in a car as ostentatious as Alexis's Porsche. I park as close as I can to the front door, then run inside, rushing up the stairs four steps at a time, and hurry into Benjamin's room.

Only a mother could understand, to see it, to forgive it. I walk around in circles, ruffling my hair, eaten away by anxiety as I open the closets, as I search everywhere. Nothing under the piles of clothes, nothing under the furniture, nothing on it. I empty the desk, filled with office supplies and childish treasures: scraps of paper, a marble, pieces of colored plastic. I turn over the bed, empty the bookshelves. Then I turn to a tray filled with drawing paper. I empty it entirely, and right there at the bottom is a tidy pile of papers.

The missing chapters.

Benjamin always considered his father's desk a playground. He would filch sheets of paper from his father, and Marceau never said anything. This time, however, Benjamin must have read the pages and was so frightened he decided he had to protect his father. Crazy how he takes after his dad, hiding secrets. Maybe he was scared I would find out and his parents would fight, maybe even separate. He was also terrified that something would break the family apart, though he'd never admit it. Instead, his fears have translated into stammering when his father died. I feel sick.

Now, sitting on my son's bed, I resume the reading that was interrupted on the boat.

The part I'm holding in my hands seems to correspond to the chapter entitled, "The accident by the lake."

It was a month before Jade disappeared. Alexis, Rollin, Jade, and I went to the twentieth birthday party of a friend of ours. A vast family property on the shore of the lake. There was one party after another that year, each one rivaling the other in excess.

Everything was good that June night. The party overflowed onto the terraces. I had drunk a lot, like many of my friends, who were starting to quarrel for no reason. Jade could feel things turning sour. She had me try to step in, but I could hardly keep upright. She called the end of the night for the four of us at around two in the morning, about half an hour after one of the troublemakers had been thrown out of the party. I was incapable of driving. Jade, who didn't have her license yet, entrusted the keys to Rollin, who was the least intoxicated of us. Alexis proclaimed that he was also perfectly capable of taking the wheel. I was lying in the back of the car, my head in Jade's lap. Rollin zigzagged along the road beside the lake while Alexis, sitting next to him, kept pretending to grab the wheel.

Suddenly, for a fraction of a second, a bicycle with no lights appeared in the headlights.

We were going slowly, but at that moment Rollin wasn't looking straight ahead, and Alexis's movement at the wheel made the car hit the bike, propelling the cyclist into a ravine that leads into the lake. Rollin quickly stopped the car. We were all in terrible shock. Rollin and Alexis sobered up very quickly. I was still in a bit of a daze. I sensed the panic sweeping over us, without understanding completely what was at stake.

Alexis ordered Rollin to drive on. We were drunk; the guy on his bicycle was almost certainly drunk too. He would sober up the next day. He probably hadn't seen what happened anyway, given how dark it was. And the car was probably fine. At worst, Alexis knew how to repair a dent and could do it himself.

The next day there was a short article in the newspaper about a cyclist found on the shore of the lake, with a high level of alcohol still in his blood. He had apparently fallen off his bike and slid over the stony embankment down to the pebble shore. We learned through some of the people from the night before that it was the guy who'd been thrown out of the party. He'd stolen the bike as he left, maybe without even realizing what he was doing. At the moment, he was in a coma. We digested this news as best we could, but for Jade, it triggered the reawakening of a deeper trauma.

She opened up about it to me. Her conscience couldn't take one more thing to be guilty about. I was scared for the two of us, scared that she would tell someone everything, especially about our father's accident. Again, I begged her to keep all of it to herself. And besides, she wasn't even at the wheel . . .

I search my memory, and I can remember news of the bike accident, though my memory is very vague. But I know things didn't end there. I wasn't there, but the police questioned everybody who was at the party.

Including the four of them. And they all kept silent.

I suddenly feel dizzy. I lean against the wall and close my eyes for a few seconds.

I turn the page and come to the chapter Marceau entitled, "The disappearance of Jade."

One month after the accident, we all went for a trek in the mountains. Several days of walking, spending the night in huts or camping out. On the morning of the third day, we heard on a radio at one of the huts that the cyclist, who'd been in a coma all that time, had just died. Jade sank into a deep silence for the rest of the day.

When night fell, as we were preparing to set up camp, she

vanished into the forest. We did everything we could to find her before it got completely dark, but she was nowhere to be found. At least that is what I told Alexis, Rollin, and Sarah, who were all worried sick.

But I had found her.

I had found Jade hanging from the branch of a tree, near a narrow, mostly unused path. She had used her climbing gear. I was so angry at myself, and I still am. By forcing her to say nothing for all those years, I had let the remorse overwhelm her while telling myself I was protecting her—protecting us. She couldn't bear it, so she put an end to her life.

That crime is mine. I didn't want to tarnish her memory and—above all—I wanted to be able to think she was alive, that she would remain alive as long as everyone kept the hope that she would come back home.

I'm very familiar with the forests, the mountains, the routes we took. I hid the body, first of all in the bed of the river, down near the waterfalls where I sometimes fished. I wedged her body among a bunch of stones, in a place that's nearly three feet deep. She was safe from everything and everyone, even from the dogs searching for her during the first days of the investigation.

When the dogs were called off and the search wrapped up, I found her a more appropriate resting place, buried in a place nobody will ever uncover unless they decode the secrets encrypted on the spines of my novels.

The story is moving—Marceau can describe these scenes better than anyone—but one huge detail doesn't fit.

Jade didn't die by hanging, like he might have thought when he discovered her.

You can't hang yourself when your legs and an arm are broken.

51

Through the window of Benjamin's bedroom, I see the reporters and police officers still bustling outside the house. I scroll through the unread texts on my phone. There are several from Karen.

> Children OK.

Then another text letting me know I have her support, and then her last text . . . that sets off all my alarm bells.

I put the two chapters down, determined to clean up this mess all by myself.

~

Hearing the engine of the Porsche start up, the reporters move aside of their own accord. As I pass, I happen to catch sight of one of the police officers take out his phone to make a call as I pass. I floor the Porsche and get to Yvoire faster than I ever have before, and hurry into the agency without greeting Karen, who's surprised to see me. I grab the keys to one of the boats, run to the dock, jump in the boat, and cast off. I'm on the hunt.

On my phone I track the location of the boat borrowed by Rollin and Alexis. They've had quite a head start on me, and they're moored somewhere near Morges, on the Swiss side of the lake. I push the boat to its maximum speed across the lake and grab a box of distress flares from the cabin. I load the flare gun and put two extra in my pockets, one in each. The flares can travel over 150 yards in a second. At close range, they would cut through a man, burning his insides. That strikes me as perfect.

Soon, I spot the agency's boat, poorly moored, as I approach the Swiss side. I make a wide turn, creating a large wave as I do, come alongside, scraping the hull of my boat against the other boat, and aim the flare gun, ready to shoot the first person I see come out. But there's no movement. The boat is empty. I moor my boat and leap onto the other one. Nothing in the cabin. I climb onto the dock, then walk along the shore, searching every possible hiding place. Could it be a trap?

Farther along the shore, I hear a noise coming from behind the gutted hull of an old boat that's been turned on its side. I see two feet sticking out, then Rollin's face. He's sitting there, looking as wretched as I've ever seen him. He nauseates me. My finger is tense on the trigger of the flare gun. I quickly look around.

"Where's Alexis? Answer me, damn it! Where is the son of a bitch?"

Rollins starts sniveling and won't stop, unable to give me a straight answer. If he's trying to trick me, I'll kill him here and now.

"He's gone, Sarah," he says at last. "He left about an hour ago."

"What about you?"

He snivels again. "I couldn't. I've had enough. Enough."

"The bastard's not going to get away with it, and neither are you! The two of you killed Jade and Marceau, and that poor guy on his bike! Admit it, for fuck's sake, admit it! I want to know what you did, everything you did!"

The flare gun is starting to weigh on my arm, and my index finger is getting stiff. I feel like hitting him, hearing him scream. I want to hear him say he's sorry for all the harm he and his pal Alexis have done, to me, to my children, to everyone. The sound of a motor comes from behind me. I glance around. Reynaud's boat.

He jumps onto the landing stage, followed by Delmas and another officer.

"Sarah! Sarah, stop! Drop the gun!"

Reynaud advances, signaling to Delmas to stay out of this. I understand what they want me to do, but right now I just want to shoot at least one of the men responsible. I want him to pay the price, and—above all—I want him to see it coming. I want him to be so scared that he shits himself before dying in excruciating pain. There's only one kind of justice for bastards like this, the kind you dispense on the spot. Twenty years is long enough to wait, isn't it?

I aim the barrel straight at Rollin, my arm outstretched.

"Look at me! Look me in the eyes, you son of a bitch!"

Rollin lifts his head and gives me a pathetic look. I press the trigger. The flare goes off and lights up an area about six feet from him. I turned the barrel aside at the last moment, but I hope the fear I've instilled in him will make clear what he's done until the day he takes his last breath. If Benjamin and Hermione hadn't been in my mind and in my heart at that moment, I would have blown his head off, with the police watching.

Reynaud comes next to me and gently takes the flare gun out of my hands. I bury my face in his shoulder to stifle my sobs. Delmas tried to lift Rollin, who has fainted. When he comes to, we bombard him with questions about Alexis.

"He's gone," he mutters. "A guy came to help him, a henchman of his best customer, I think. He had a car. I didn't want to follow him, so he left on his own."

Delmas walks away to make a series of phone calls. Roadblocks have been set up everywhere, and an international arrest warrant has been issued.

Rollin continues answering questions.

"Alexis has contacts everywhere. He can easily get papers; he can get a private plane. He's probably already in the air and across the mountains. He's been preparing our escape ever since the investigation started."

Delmas curses.

"That scumbag isn't going to slip through our fingers."

Reynaud turns to him.

"It took me twenty years to find the body I'd been searching for desperately. So, I wish you luck."

I free myself from Reynaud's embrace. He looks at me anxiously. I shake my head. My wave of rage and madness has dissipated. Reynaud replaces Delmas in questioning Rollin. The sudden cooperation of these two police officers who've been at each other's throats is almost touching.

"Rollin," he says softly, "can you tell me how all this mess started?"

Rollin has a little color returning to his face. He may also look better now that he's confessing everything, now that he no longer needs to run.

"It was during the last book party at your house, Sarah. When I got soaked by the automatic sprinkler and I went inside to dry myself and borrow some clothes from Marceau. Once I'd changed, I stopped for a few moments in his study. It was the first time I'd been in there, you know how he was. There's something special about the study of a famous writer. Marceau was always very silent about his work, even with us, his best friends. I took advantage of the opportunity and looked around, getting a feel of his private world, and that is when I came across . . ." He's sniveling again. "The climbing clip . . ."

Reynaud places a hand on his shoulder to stop him shaking. "What climbing clip? What do you mean?"

"We all had a climbing clip—a carabiner—with our name engraved on it. I lost mine somewhere years ago. You had one too, Sarah. But the clip I found on Marceau's desk was Jade's. Marceau came into the study as I was holding it in my hand. That piece of metal was proof that Marceau had found Jade's body."

He looks away but seems ready to tell us everything.

"Jade had been hanged . . . with that clip, her clip. It was Alexis and me . . . to make it look like a suicide. When we pushed her from an overhang. She wanted to reveal everything about the accident, about the guy on the bike that we'd hit and left to die. We were responsible for it, and Marceau *had* to believe that his sister had killed herself. That was what we hoped at the time. Then, on the evening of the party, when Marceau found me in his study with the clip, he looked me straight in the eyes and ordered me to leave the room immediately and not to touch his stuff ever again. He told me he was writing everything that happened down. I got scared, and I immediately told Alexis . . . and Alexis decided . . . we had to silence him. And we had to take his computer, the backups, the memory sticks, everything to stop the truth from coming out."

I'm stunned. I'm sorry I didn't just kill him when I had the chance.

"So Marceau died feeling guilty for his sister's suicide, when it was you who killed her and disguised her death! You killed Jade . . . and Marceau! How could you—"

Delmas cuts me off. He fills in the last shadowy areas of the macabre puzzle.

"If the manuscript had been found, we'd have known why Jade was feeling so bad, about the hit-and-run, and above all, we'd have been able to find her body and proof that she'd been murdered. So, you had to kill the one person capable of exposing you."

"But I'm the one who found the manuscript," I say. "It almost slipped through my fingers. Marceau was good at hiding things, even from me, his wife—and even after his death."

Rollin is sitting huddled on the ground. I'm itching to kick him. I start remembering other things. This bastard hasn't spat it all out yet.

"I thought I was going crazy," I say. "That feeling I was constantly being watched. Was that you or was it Alexis? Answer me!"

Rollin moans. Reynaud puts a hand on my arm, as if to stop me doing something I might regret.

At last, Rollin blurts it out.

"Alexis went berserk when he saw how determined you were to get hold of that manuscript. He wanted to make you feel crazy so that you'd stop searching."

"When I almost drowned in the middle of the night, was he there? And Benjamin's coat in the forest, was that him or you? What about the dead fish in my pickup? Was that you, my old friends?"

Delmas and Reynaud are so astonished they no longer dare to intervene.

"Alexis was obsessed by everything you were doing," Rollin whines. "He asked me to do other things too, but it got to be impossible for me in the end . . ."

Emerging from his shock, Reynaud takes a step toward Rollin, as if to get between him and me. "Other things like what, Rollin?"

Rollin starts sniveling again.

"The password to the agency's computer. He asked me to go there during Karen's lunch hour. I knew it hadn't changed since I'd helped to install the system. I have duplicate keys to the agency. Karen had started doubting you too."

This time, Reynaud really does have to hold me back from strangling Rollin.

Delmas resumes the interrogation. "Where is the computer? And the backup?"

"Alexis gave me the necessary references, plus a little extra money, to hand them to one of the guys I was dealing drugs with. The guy immediately found the equipment. But it was Alexis who handled things in your house, Sarah, destroying Marceau's computer and replacing it with a new one while you were out at the office or driving around in your pickup."

"Everyone was looking for Marceau, and you knew he was already dead? You make me sick."

I suddenly remember another detail that might make sense now.

"What about Louise's diaries?"

He sighs, as if he dreads what he still has to say. He doesn't even have the courage to show any dignity now that he's been unmasked.

"When Karen told me your grandmother Louise wrote everything down in those notebooks of hers, I got scared. I knew Marceau went to see her regularly. A guy who comes to the food truck works over there, and I gave him some money to get hold of the books . . . and . . . I burned them."

"They were my grandmother's precious memories, the most intimate thing she had."

Reynaud again takes over, with a question that's particularly dear to him since he was in custody.

"They found a sling near the summit. It belonged to the Forest Center."

Rollin scratches nervously at the ground, his head down. "The sling . . . That was Alexis . . . He wanted to secure himself, to make sure he didn't fall when he threw the stone at you. I found the sling lying next to Zoé's bike in our garage. She used it to carry her things."

"What about my gun?" Reynaud asked.

"One day, Marceau showed us the gun he'd borrowed from you. We did a bit of shooting with it. He kept it away from the house because of the children, but Alexis knew where it was hidden. He put it in Marceau's study, in a place where the cops would find it, just to draw attention to his surprising and possibly dangerous behavior."

"Except that I'm the one who found it," I cut in. "Alexis didn't foresee that. But that didn't change any of your plans, not really, apart from the extra collateral damage . . . And on the Dent du Vélan, who shot at me in the forest?"

Incredulous, Reynaud and Delmas exchange glances. They're only now realizing what I've gone through these past few weeks. And so am I, I admit. I feel as if I'm in a waking dream. Rollin hides his face in his hands. His voice is so muffled, we can barely hear him.

"I told Alexis that was going too far. I couldn't stand it anymore. He just wanted to scare you. He thought he loved you and was angry at himself . . . at least, I think so."

The son of a bitch even slept with me . . . He disgusts me, I disgust myself. Was that also part of his plan to manipulate me, or was he pitifully trying to apologize for all the horror he'd done?

Delmas signals to us to stop. He looks pretty disgusted himself. He strikes the final blow.

"You're going to prison, Rollin Uldry, for a long time. As for your accomplice, we'll catch him soon enough."

52

THE MANUSCRIPT

When you're a novelist, it's hard to imagine the day will come when you write your final book. There's always tomorrow; there's always a new story, one you're carrying inside you even before you've finished the previous one. The Story of Marceau Miller *will inevitably be my last. In a way, it forces you to think twice before writing the words "the end." And I'm lucky that I can revise what I write as many times as I feel the need, until* my *end. That's a writer's job, constantly revising his work.*

This story is the first I won't see arrive in the hands of those it's meant for.

So, I can say everything, even the unmentionable, even the unforgivable.

I won't be here when these lines are read, but my conscience will have delivered what it had to: the truth.

The End

EPILOGUE

THREE MONTHS LATER

The morning light has always been my favorite. It makes you feel that everything is still possible. The lake is even more beautiful in the glow of the rising sun—Louise was right. Reynaud carried out her last wish for me. "I'd like all my pebbles to go back into the lake." There were 529 pebbles, all numbered, with a combined weight of 250 pounds, which Reynaud took on board his boat and released to the bottom of the lake. Goodbye, Granny Louise. I only have a few of her diaries, and in them I've discovered a few more of Marceau's secrets.

Like him, she wrote everything down.

Now I'm driving the pickup to the agency for the last time, a pang in my heart. You only become free when you let go once and for all. I'm going to cut through the ties with an axe in one fell swoop.

Moored at the dock, two boats are bobbing up and down on the lake. The others have been hired and are out somewhere on the lake between France and Switzerland.

I advance toward the agency, determined. Karen is behind the counter, keeping her distance. I must do this quickly, efficiently, without emotion, which is, I'm sure, what she's hoping for. It's been three months since the case was wrapped up, three months since we last saw each other. I'm selling her my shares in the agency. She hasn't had a chance to say a word, either about my decision or about the price, which was high. But there are some prices that can't be negotiated.

Karen can't look me in the face. The cracks in her perfection make me feel a little less nervous. She looks like she'd break into pieces if I touched her, and she knows I can see that. I sign the papers she's prepared. She looks up at me, with what courage she has left.

"Sarah, it only happened a few times with Marceau. It was a time when he was lost. He was the one who put an end to it. I'm so sorry . . ."

She has stolen a little bit of my husband, taken the other half of our agency, and has lost all of my trust.

I have one last surprise for her, which I take out of my bag, gift wrapped in black paper and tied with a red ribbon. The black of death, the red of blood. I put it down on top of the contracts. The first copy of Marceau's last book.

"Now you have the complete collection. But there's no dedication this time. He says hello from wherever he is now."

I sense her recoil, which is enough for me before I turn on my heels and leave.

~

I wasn't present at the press conference given by Édouard, but I'm sure he quite enjoyed it. I don't know if it's out of respect or out of sincere friendship, but he's kept the original title of the manuscript, *The Story of Marceau Miller*. The true story of his life with all its shadows and its share of darkness. As if he's thumbing his nose at a career corrupted by lies. The border between reality and fiction can blur until they are lost—or found.

I gave Édouard permission to publish the manuscript because Marceau wanted the truth to be known, and without this book, it would be impossible for me to ever feel free. Not that I'll ever be able to rid myself of this story completely. It's inked into the skin of my ankle, at least part of it, its beginning. What Jade wanted.

And what now? Should I leave? Maybe go somewhere else rather than stay in the home, the area that is—always has been—our home?

In the windows of all the bookstores I pass, I see *The Story of Marceau Miller*. Some copies have little notes from the booksellers, like signposts helping me to say:

Goodbye, Marceau.

ACKNOWLEDGMENTS

My heartfelt thanks to:

My first reader, Sophie, and my daughters, who from the start have supported my passions and literary projects.

Marie Leroy, my trusted publisher, who can read between my lines, with whom the days and nights spent working on a manuscript sometimes blend into one another—for the better, we hope.

My agent, Michèle Kanonidis, who supports me and opens up new vistas beyond the borders of our country.

My international agent, Marleen Seegers, who, even during her flights over oceans and countries, finds the energy to give me valuable comments on the manuscript.

Geneviève Perrin, the publisher who trusted me all those years ago and still gives me valuable advice.

My readers, for whom I've had enormous pleasure writing this story and experiencing some truly intense emotions.